THE FRUITCAKE

Four friends, one fruitcake, and a
ritzy town full of secrets...What could go wrong?

LEAH ORR

Pre-release Praise
From Readers with Advanced Reader Copies
The Fruitcake

I had an hour to kill, so I started reading this book - 5 hours later, I raced out of bed to check the back slider to ensure it was locked! - Mary H.

An unputdownable thriller. - George K.

An ending I did not see coming. - Amanda G.

Initially, it seems like you're reading two separate stories, then BAM! Now, I question everything I read and have to flip back through the pages to find all the clues I missed. - Joy A.

I'm never eating fruitcake again. - Paul P.

I'm gifting this book to my sister this Christmas instead of bringing a fruitcake - Simone B.

An original thriller with an excellent storyline that keeps you guessing until the end. - Gary M.

Lock your doors, don't eat the fruitcake, and don't trust your neighbors! - Alana A.

This book is a work of fiction. While some of the people and places are real, all of the characters, organizations, businesses, and events portrayed in this book are used fictitiously.

This book is printed in the USA.

The Fruitcake. Copyright 2022 by Leah Orr.
All rights reserved.
Cover art by Deposit photos. Photographer VlaDee.
Fruitcake art by Josephine Lepore.

Library of Congress Control Number: 2023919017

First Edition October 31, 2023
ISBN Paperback 979-8-9855783-8-6
ISBN Hardcover 979-8-9855783-9-3
ISBN Ebook 979-8-9855783-7-9

Leah Orr
Jensen Beach, Florida
Orrplace Press
Distributed by IngramSpark/Lightning Source

In a book club? Want signed copies?
Contact Leah directly at:
www.leahorr.com
Or by email:
orrplace1@bellsouth.net

Dedicated to my brother Rico

The Fruitcake

Leah Orr

In the end . . . we all
get what we deserve.

Prologue

Christmas Eve
2022 6:45 a.m.
Holly

T he ancient Romans were a bunch of assholes. This is the only clear thought milling around my head at this ungodly morning hour as I trek across the cul-de-sac with this ridiculous fruitcake. The Romans, who once ate fruitcake to sustain themselves in battle, are currently the focus of my ire. If I could piss on their graves, surely I would for upending my life right now.

The fruitcake exchange infiltrated my neighborhood, Laguna Palms, circa 2018. It was a foolish idea that Patty, a neighbor and illustrious HOA president at the time, initiated. A neighbor was selected to bring good tidings to another with a homemade fruitcake. The following year, *that* neighbor would bake their version of a fruitcake and gift it to another family.

This year, it's my turn. I wish I never agreed to participate in this absurd tradition. Good tidings for the new year? Bullshit! This year, the incoming HOA hag, Sandra, suggested, or should I say, demanded in a passive-aggressive way that I deliver a fruitcake to the Hudson sisters.

I don't care for Sandra to be candid. She doesn't wear makeup. I don't trust women who don't wear makeup. In my opinion, they're lazy. They don't have much respect for themselves or the rest of the world, who have to look at them. The lack of makeup is bad enough, but the long black chin hairs dancing about while she speaks make it so much worse. It's difficult not to stare. Don't judge me—I'm just trying to be honest. Few people are these days.

"Don't you think it would be a great idea to gift the fruitcake to the Hudson sisters?" ugly Sandra suggested. "They rarely set foot outside of their home. Wouldn't it be a nice gesture from the community to bestow good graces upon them this year?" Her puny eyes twinkled in delight like she just invented a laundry-folding robot and was thrilled to tell me all about it. Her eyes, mind you, would be better represented with a bit of mascara, but I digress.

Well, I'd rather have a pap smear, I thought. But what I actually said was, "Sure." My first instinct is always to be polite.

Eff this ridiculous tradition. I've never even met the Hudson sisters. Now I have to bake them a cake? I say "eff" only because I'm trying to tamp down on my swearing. These days, my colorful language is out of control. Just quitting the really bad words, however, not the fun little ones. I deserve *some* joy in my life. In my defense, wouldn't most people have a few choice words when raising triplet seven-year-olds? Most definitely, if they were raising my "fantastic beasts." This, a Harry Potter prequel reference I most enjoy, as I picture my children as magical creatures, stampeding out from the bottomless suitcase of the magical zoologist wizard known as Newt.

I decided to make a Havana fruitcake. A recipe my grandfather passed down from his relatives in Cuba.

I nearly dropped this yucky candied creation twice en route to the Hudson sisters. Once when an agama lizard, an invasive species trying to take over control of my neighborhood, scurries across my feet in the driveway, and again when the seventeen-year-old living across from me, Chet, pops up out of nowhere, dog on leash, calling out, "Good morning, Mrs. Kelly!"

I whirl around, startled. The cake nearly slides off the Christmas plate decorated with dancing elves, and I let out a soft, barely audible scream.

Chet, looking amused, asks, "Are you alright, Mrs. Kelly? Um, Holly . . . can I help you?" His eyes now fixate on my breasts, and then . . . he winks at me.

Did he just wink at me? Call me by my first name? Such a creepy, skinny little shit. His goatee and gross, wiry mustache are repulsive. No wonder he possesses no female attention and few friends.

"No, Chet. I'm fine," I say, trying my best to be pleasant. "Just try not to sneak up on people so early in the morning. You nearly gave me a heart attack."

"Sorry, ma'am," he says. But he was not. He smiles, turns away, and off he goes toward the neighborhood dog park.

Still dark, broad gusts of light shine from streetlights. "Good flippin' morning," I mutter out loud to myself, smiling slightly, proud of myself for not swearing. These polite rituals should be banned before the sun rises. No one should wake before the sun, in my opinion. It's barbaric.

Nevertheless, here I am delivering this dastardly nut-filled, joyless fruitcake slathered in cream cheese icing, attempting to create the illusion that what you are about to eat may actually be delectable. I even added Hershey's chocolate syrup and strawberries atop for panache. Try as I may, a fruitcake is simply disgusting.

I walk faster now, determined to complete my mission. Because I gave my driver the day off, soon *I* will have to drive my kids to the Children's Museum for a half-day Christmas celebration. While most parents won't bring their kids to this particular holiday activity, any time away from my little cretins is a gift I will accept gleefully.

The Hudson sisters probably won't even eat this shitty cake; strange characters, those two. One is fat—again, I ask, don't judge me. It's the only way to describe her accurately. A three-hundred-pound guesstimate would be kind. A real *chalupa*, my Mexican friends from Miami would say. The other, short and dumpy-looking, never looks freshly showered. I have only seen them a handful of times, rolling out the garbage cans or collecting their mail. I hear they work at the Martin County jail. I'm not surprised. They look exactly like typical prison guards in movies. They get visitors from time to time, but they seldom stay long.

Birds are singing louder than usual, and two bunnies jump out from the flowering shrubs as I approach the Hudson house.

"Hello, bunnies," I say. "I know what you were doing in that planter, and in a few weeks, I am sure I will see five or more of you—unless the bobcat gets to you first."

I look up momentarily and notice that their home has one of those clear glass entrance doors that allows you to see directly into the house through to the backyard and sand dunes beyond the fence line. This is captivating in magazines but not practical in real life. Who wants to live in a way where you can't lounge around every once in a while in your pajamas, or have the ability to hide from those wretched Jehovah's Witnesses, spreading their warped ideas of imminent hellfire and Armageddon. What's worse are those pesky, ponytailed but super-cute Girl Scouts toting their two-thousand-calorie cookies that I can't control myself from eating. It's a bit of an exaggeration, but you get the point.

Head down, I climb the steps to the entrance door—one . . . two . . . three . . . four . . . five . . . six . . . and seven. Counting steps: an annoying habit I can't seem to kick, but it helps to ease my anxiety, which always tends to creep in during unexpected situations. When I reach the top of the stairs, I raise my head to ring the doorbell.

I am met with a piercing scream. One of the Hudson sisters, the obese one, is gripping a bloody man's head with her left hand as he frantically tries to crawl away. Another scream, and then another, comes muffled from elsewhere in the house. I can't tell where the other screams are coming from.

Unaware of my presence at the front door, the Hudson sister slings a small, sharp hatchet into the man's skull with her right hand, spraying blood across the floor, the walls, and her face. Her face . . . the rage. His face . . . the fear. Before he was struck, those few milliseconds will linger in my mind forever, watching me arrive and peer inside. He looked directly at me. His eyes, pleading with me, terrified . . . desperate for help. But I can't help him now. It's too late for that.

My heart races. Hands jittery, I drop the fruitcake, which stays intact, unsurprisingly, save a few strawberries that roll off on their own. The Christmas plate, however, shatters into countless itty-bitty pieces against the pavers below, dancing elves eviscerated, murdered.

I turn and run past the bunnies, the birds, the lizard, and Chet. All of these creatures tried in their own way—obstacles in my path—to keep me away this morning.

"Fuck, fuck, fuck!" I scream out as I sprint toward home. My swearing is necessary this time, as only those words will suffice. I race into the house and lock the door.

Three little sets of eyes at the breakfast table stare inquisitively in my direction. Hundreds of Froot Loops decorate the kitchen table. That reckless trio emptied the entire cereal box while I stepped away for ten minutes. To be expected, I suppose. They watch me curiously in my frantic state but say nothing. Their interests lie solely in playing with their sugary mini circles and colorful crumbs that spilled out from the bottom of the bag.

My heart still racing; I take a deep breath, grab my cell phone from the counter, and dial 911.

"Hello . . . please send help . . . right now! I just witnessed a murder."

Part One

Laguna Palms:

The Neighbors, the Capture, and the Fruitcake

2018–2023

Chapter One

Laguna Palms
July 2018
Holly

Do you find a place, or does a place find you? A special feeling is provoked when you initially drive into a neighborhood, or walk through a house that you know instinctively you must have—the feeling of *home*. You can't accurately explain the scent of it, but if you could bottle it and create a perfume or candle, you'd be rich. Home is a feeling, an instinct, a sense of belonging, like you have finally found your place in the world. A comfortable place where you can just be you. Suddenly, a metaphorical weight lifts. You feel lighter. A childish giddiness kicks in, and a new chapter unfolds.

Everyone in this community belongs here in some way or another. We were all drawn here for different reasons and from different walks of life, but our fates have intertwined purposefully in a way that can't be explained until years have passed and you can reflect upon it with the wisdom that only hindsight provides.

Laguna Palms is a five-hundred-acre private, gated sanctuary located on Hutchinson Island in Florida. It's situated between the St. Lucie Inlet and the Atlantic Ocean. This little piece of paradise has its own marina, fitness center, clubhouse, dog park, golf course, tennis and pickleball courts, and two miles of white sandy beaches.

One of the more popular attractions is a small shopping center with must-have shops such as Starbucks, a Whole Foods Market convenience store, and Lululemon because what woman can live without the comfort of a perfectly cozy pair of leggings? A warm, snug hug for our legs that we wear to the gym, casually throughout the day, and can easily transition to evening attire. A must-have for ladies of the Florida south. How else could you combine mindfulness, sweat, community, comfort, and fashion in just one product—truly revolutionary. In my opinion, however, Athleta leggings are just as good or better—a secret just between us.

The nearly five hundred residents here are not just affluent; they're resourceful, astute, next-generation entrepreneurs, and forward thinkers. You won't get into any arguments around here about the geometric shape of the planet. Outside these gates—well, it's Florida… never been known to be the brightest of the bunch.

The residents also possess copious disposable cash to burn. How else could one afford the $75,000 capital nonrefundable one-time contribution for new homeowners and the annual $26,000 HOA fees, not including a typical $15,000 annual assessment for community renovations? In addition, lest we not forget, there's the $5,000 commitment to dine and entertain at the clubhouse, a $3,500 fee for dry boat storage at the marina, and last but not least, a measly $1,200 annual trail fee to use your private golf cart on the course.

While the surrounding condominiums and communities along the Hutchinson shores attract retirees, this community thrives on a more social, agile, and wealthier clientele.

Our salesperson at the time—Adam or Andy or some a-hole whose name I can't remember—says, "You know, over nine hundred people, like yourselves, move to Florida every day."

"Is that right?" I say to play along like Bradley and I didn't already know this widely-known fact about Florida. Between his smug demeanor, slimy-slick hairdo that went out of style in the late fifties, and how he only addresses my husband instead of me, he is beginning to piss me off.

Bradley is a man's man. I get it. He's hard to look away from. He stands confidently at six feet three inches tall, and he's fit like he belongs on the cover of *Men's Health* magazine. He commands attention with only his presence, like a celebrity.

The sales creep swoons about, smiling, getting lost in my husband's dreamy hazel eyes. He's flirting with him. It's obvious. This wormy little snake is giddy with the prospect of selling a home to my sexy husband as if it wasn't *my* decision to move here in the first place. He's really getting under my skin, rubbing me in all the wrong ways.

"Well, we are *from* Florida. Miami, Florida," I say.

He looks me over, head to toe, sizing me up like I don't matter. I cringe. He says, "Miami is like another country compared to Hutchinson Island. Most people *here* speak English."

"Is that so?" Now I'm annoyed and angry. I can feel my body temperature elevate. I bore my nails into the palm of my hand to divert my anguish elsewhere. I nearly draw blood. My husband squeezes my other hand, a gesture between us that means *play nice*.

"Florida is paradise, and Laguna Palms living on Hutchinson Island is pure heaven," the sleazy salesman boasts, looking square into my husband's eyes with a crooked, creepy smile.

"Or just a sunny place for shady people," I quip, thinking of a familiar adage: Behind every successful fortune, there is a crime. I'm not sure who originally said this, but the quote is common in mob movies my husband loves to watch.

"Prepare the paperwork. We'd like to move in within a month." Bradley extends his hand toward the creepy home peddler for a final shake, pushing the conversation quickly toward its conclusion. Then the salesman reaches for my hand to shake as well.

Instead, I turn abruptly and walk away. "Adios, muchacho," I blurt out, waving my injured hand over my head. Then, under my breath, I utter, "*Come mierda!*" That literally means, "Eat shit," for all you gringos out there. Suddenly, I remember it was Mario Puzo, the author of *The Godfather*, who said, "Behind every successful fortune, there is a crime." I knew it would come back to me eventually.

We moved into Laguna Palms in the fall of 2018. Bradley, a music producer for Sony Music Entertainment, spends most of the month traveling. We fell in love with this neighborhood. Not because of Adam/Andy/Asshole, but rather the social activity and waterfront location. I would surely make friends here in my five-thousand-square-foot McMansion on the seashore while he travels. This was one of the driving ideas for the move to paradise—a bright, sunshiny community. But, as they say, not every shiny thing is golden.

Chapter Two

Meeting Gina
August 2018
Holly

Friendship is truly one of the great joys in life. I would argue that it's even more important or just as necessary as the spouse you choose. Friends increase your sense of belonging and purpose, boost your happiness, improve self-confidence and self-worth, and help you cope with trauma. The best part is that they're cheaper than therapists. Good ones teeter the imaginary line between truth and deceit masterfully. They must be brave enough to say all the painful things that will be hard to hear. And at the same time, can paint a perfect little white lie in just the right way to make you feel invincible: "Dump that guy! He's an asshole. You can do better!" But also: "Sure, the red dress is lovely, but wear the black dress instead. It's the most figure-flattering for your curves." Finding that fifty-fifty friendship is rare and should be cherished.

A very tall woman with a cane, already standing in the middle of her front walkway, calls out the very moment Bradley and I step out of the house to greet the moving van.

"Hello, neighbors! Aren't you two precious? Such a cute couple. Where are you two from?"

Stepping off the steps onto the walkway, I say, "Miami."

She offers me a smile. "What brings you so far north? Must be a hundred and twenty miles or so away," she says, anxiously awaiting my answer.

"Well, I hear the island has become a hotspot for raising children these days," I lie. This is not an accurate statement at all. Few children live on the island, as most families with small children live over the bridge in Jensen Beach or Stuart.

I can see she is not ready to understand my level of sarcasm, as we have just met. Her false eyelashes flutter. Her face contorts, eyebrows raise, and she shakes her head slightly like she wants to tell me I'm wrong, but chooses instead to continue our polite conversation.

Suddenly, my three kiddos race past in a flurry of excitement to watch a platoon of movers arrive, armed with furniture straps and ready for battle. When Bradley excuses himself to drive to the grocery store, the woman slowly inches closer toward me. Sunlight caught in her messy bun, she saunters over impressively with an elegant ease you wouldn't expect from a woman dependent upon a cane.

"I'm sorry, let me introduce myself. I'm Gina." Her tone stays light and airy, determined to keep things pleasant. "To welcome you to the neighborhood, I took it upon myself to create an illustration of the homes in the cul-de-sac with everyone's names to help you get acclimated." She hands me an index-sized card out of the side pocket of her leggings.

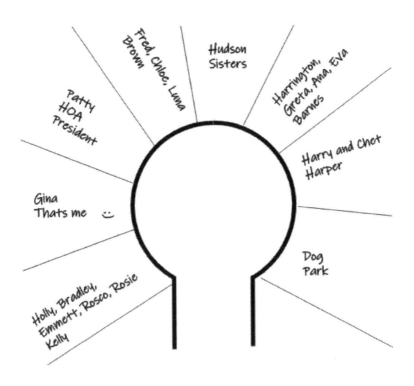

"Thank you very much. That's very thoughtful," I say while observing the note card. "It's nice to meet you, Gina. I'm Holly. My husband is Bradley, and our kids: Rosco, Emmett, and Rosie." I point toward the kids while sneaking another peak at the makeshift map she created for me.

"You already have me entered, I see."

"Yes. Patty, our HOA president, who lives beside me, told me you were moving in today."

"Oh, nice."

"How old are your kids?" She gestures toward my little runaways.

"They are three, turning four in February," I answer.

"They are quick on their feet for three-year-olds."

"Yes, they are. Quick to learn everything."

"Must be difficult raising triplets."

"You wouldn't understand the half of it. They race around like a cat five hurricane."

"Well, we will have to sit and chat one day soon—um, I mean—once you're settled. No pressure, of course. It's been a long time since we had a new neighbor."

"Really?"

"Yes. Most people will settle in and stay for as long as they can afford to live here, which typically turns out to be five to seven years. This cul-de-sac, however, these homes just off the shoreline, usually keep their inhabitants until they die or until the IRS or FBI come knocking—a story for another day."

"Interesting . . . Well, I would be delighted to meet and chat one day soon," I say but don't mean it. Although, I'll bet some of her stories would be pretty entertaining.

"How long have you lived here?" I ask, trying to be cordial.

"Ten years. My father left me the house with his estate when he passed."

"I'm so sorry for your loss," I say, throwing out the acceptable universal response.

"Don't be. He was an ass, always working, and never paid much attention to us kids growing up. Anyway," she says, looking away at the movers hauling couches off of the semi-truck, "another long story for another time." She shrugs with a giant toothy smile like she can't wait to unleash her personal baggage and chatter about petty neighborhood gossip.

Who doesn't love a scandal? Shameful improprieties? I definitely do. She seems interesting enough, the friendly, gossipy, neighborly type you love and yet . . . also love to hate. But my initial impression is that she would be the type of woman who would embarrass you in Starbucks. The type to order a double, half-caff, blah, blah, blah, cappuccino with oat milk and extra whipped cream. You know the type. Extra. Extra. I reign in my thoughts. I have shit to do. This house will not decorate itself, and Lord knows my husband is no help at all.

"Emmett and Rosco, stop running around the oak tree," I snap. "You're going to fall. I'm sorry, Gina, those two swirl around like a freaking cyclone—can't keep up."

"I see you've got your hands full."

"Okay, then," I say. "Let me help the movers settle the furniture in the house, just in case they don't understand the blueprint I created." She clears her throat loudly as I turn around to walk back inside.

"Oh, just one other thing," she offers, pointer finger in the air. "If you need a babysitter, I'm available late afternoons and evenings. I work mostly in the morning, and I'm usually available from two o'clock on."

Now, I have to stop, turn back around, and ask the many questions swirling around in my head. What exactly do you do for a living to have so much free time? And why would any sane person ever volunteer to babysit three-year-old triplets?

"What, now?" I say, trying not to show my sudden shock. "You would like to babysit? Really? I'll have to keep that in mind. Thank you. Why after two? What do you do for a living? If you don't mind me asking. Are you a schoolteacher?"

"Well . . ." She pauses, then blurts out, "I am a foot fetish model." She lifts her head proudly.

Shocked by her cavalier admittance, my jaw falls open slightly. "Oh, fascinating . . . I'm going to have to hear more about that." Now, I am really going to make sure I carve out time for a friendly visit. This is captivating.

"I prefer to think of myself as a social influencer," she goes on. "While most influencers are young travelers, foodies, dance enthusiasts, or fashionistas, my so-called claim to fame is my feet."

"Your feet?" She has my full attention now.

"Yes, I am—or was—a runway model." And this, I can believe. She stands over six feet tall, by my best guess. I never feel short, but I feel tiny with my five-foot-six frame beside hers.

"A back injury took me out of the game. Now I walk with a bit of a limp," she says, gesturing toward her cane. "But my feet have netted me a few million over the past five years over social media."

"Holy shit!" The words slip out without my permission. The movers are interrupting, asking me questions. I can barely pay attention long enough to tell them where the stupid couches must go. I motioned them toward the living room and honestly couldn't give a shit where they put them. I have to learn more about this foot fetish thing.

"I have my profile on feet finder dot com."

"That's a real thing?" Although, I shouldn't be surprised. You can find nearly anything on the web these days.

"Yes. I have people who subscribe to my channel for a monthly fee, or you can buy a photo individually if you like. Well, um, I don't mean you, but a collective you. My username is treasure coast sugar toes. All one word."

I can only imagine what she does with her gargantuan feet. My best guess is size eleven or, dare I say, twelve. Thirteen? My kids rush past me and hop onto the couches the movers just placed.

"Kids, stop jumping on the sofas!" I scream out in desperation. "I'm sorry, Gina, I have to go. I've got an avalanche of things to do." Then I say in a high, singsongy voice, "Never a boring day here in the Kelly house."

Gina laughs, then says, "That's funny."

"Funny?"

"Yes, funny. All your analogies relate to some natural disaster: hurricane, cyclone, avalanche. It's funny."

"I hadn't noticed that, but nothing exposes the truth like chaos, I presume," I say nervously.

"Alright, Gina, one day soon, after I pick up the kids from preschool, I will drop by, after two, of course, to chat further," I say, racing up the steps toward the front door to keep the kids from destroying all our worldly possessions. I can hear Gina yell back, "We have a blizzard of topics to discuss," and I smile. I am going to like this neighbor.

At seven, I put the kids to bed after singing a sweet lullaby:

> *"Sleep tight, little ones, drift away,*
> *Until the sun rises to a brand new day.*
> *Drift now, little ones, far and away,*
> *To a place, your dreams will come true one day.*
> *No matter where you go or what you do,*
> *Mommy is always here for you.*
> *Spring, summer, winter, fall,*
> *I will love you through it all."*

Emmett falls asleep right away.

"Mommy, your voice is pretty. You sound like an angel," says Rosie.

"You sound like an angel on fire." Rosco throws his hands up in the air with excitement.

"Well, that's a disturbing image. Goodnight, my loves," I say while doling out kisses for everyone.

Hours later, once the furnishings are in place and before I can revel in the comfort of my own home, I find her feet online. Damn, Gina! I found her most recent photo. Her giant feet, with painted candy apple red toenail polish, are lathered in white frosting and multicolored sprinkles. A lit candle between both feet. The title of this valuable piece of photography: *Birthday Feet*. I can download the photo for free with a recurring $100 a-month membership, or for a measly $29.99, I can purchase a single image. Yup, I bought the photo. I couldn't resist. It's now the screensaver on my Mac.

Chapter Three

Taken
December 1, 2022
The Captive

A bee sting of pain in my neck, dizziness, and oblivion was the last I could recollect as I lay here on the damp concrete floor, fluorescent lights flickering and buzzing above. My head is pounding, pants soaked in urine. What happened to me? My eyes are finding it difficult to adjust. Blink, blink, blink. I twist my neck around, trying to take in my surroundings. The air is sour and stale. What is this place? A basement? In Florida? Most importantly, why am I here?

I must have drifted off because I remember awakening to a loud thud, then silence. My ears prick, and using all my energy to listen, I hear the sound of metal on metal, a scrape of a key. A large, heavy door opens slowly, and a shadowy figure lingers in the frame. The blurry figure slides a plastic hospital tray toward me containing three small water bottles and a turkey sandwich. I hadn't realized my mouth was dry until I took a sip. My mouth stings, burning from the water it so desperately needs. How long has it been since I consumed anything? Last I remember, I drank a cup of coffee this morning before heading out for a three-mile walk, my daily ritual before heading to work.

My Apple Watch buzzes. Low battery, it warns. I get a bit excited. The watch will log an electronic footprint. Someone is sure to find me soon. I try to stay positive, but every bone in my body jolts, fearing what's to come.

The room starts to spin . . . the water . . . it must be drugged. Darkness envelopes me, and again I descend.

Chapter Four

The Neighbors
November 2018
Holly

O f course, I can't tell Gina I'm a big fan of her work. Not yet, anyway—too soon. But, to be honest, her work is delicious.

Within the next few weeks, she and I became fast friends. She may be among the most interesting people I've ever met. Although, I did have a neighbor once who was a circus tightrope walker and aerialist for the infamous Ringling Bros. and Barnum & Bailey. While gardening on the front lawn, she loved to shock the neighborhood, wearing her tiny dresses and no underwear. She often would bend over just as cars passed—especially Bradley's. She was pretty interesting. She would, however, take a distant second to Gina.

Gina has worked with and dated many cute celebrities I promised not to mention, but let me jumble up some letters and say, for example, Cradley Booper. She's also friendly with nearly everyone in the community. She has undoubtedly mastered every technique suggested by Dale Carnegie in his best-selling book *How to Win Friends and Influence People*. She is alarmingly pretty, entertaining, and completely mesmerizing, a person you couldn't forget once you met. Her gregarious personality, tall six-foot-plus frame, square jawline, perfectly sculpted cheekbones, slight limp, and Farrah Fawcett hairdo attract attention in every endeavor. She always looks perfectly put together, and the ease she emits as she walks past, even with a slight limp, makes you feel like she has not a care in the world. You want to be part of her universe.

I, on the other hand, always feel disheveled. Every piece of clothing I own is stained with the grubby little hands from my grungy trio. Don't get me wrong, I love those little buggers, but living with them is like living inside a typhoon. This makes me smile, another disaster analogy surrounding my family life.

My appearance is often bedraggled, makeup haphazardly plastered upon my face in a huff. I once had a boyfriend tell me my eyes are vomit green. We didn't date for very long. Obvi. My impossible-to-curl hair has no luster. My hair color comes from a tiny box I purchased at the local CVS. Clairol Nice'n Easy, black. Not even a fancy name like raven black, ebony, or onyx. Just a tiny box that says black. I suppose I could afford a talented colorist at a fancy salon—no doubt. In this instance, however, my frugal Miami-Cuban upbringing kicks in. Why pay a color stylist three to four hundred dollars for something I can easily do myself? The hair dye costs a paltry seven dollars and fifty-seven cents. Frankly, there is nothing quite like the satisfying sense of accomplishment from saving a few dollars—even when I don't need to.

One morning, shortly after Bradley raced out the door to enjoy some daddy time at the park with my triplet terrorists, the doorbell rang.

"Oh, Good Lord," I yell out loud to no one. I throw my hands up in the air in defiance, hoping to expel some excess anger. Just when I get a few moments of peace and quiet, I'm interrupted by the outside world. I take a deep breath and push the bad air out, calming myself down as I open the door.

"Hey girl," Gina grabs my wrist, pulling me down the steps toward her yellow convertible Porsche. "I noticed Bradley escaping with the kids, so let's grab a cup of coffee."

"Alright," I surrender. "I just need to get back before anyone misses me. Where are we going?"

"You'll see," She opens the trunk and hands me a pair of Ralph Lauren sunglasses. "For the ride. It's windy going over the bridge with the top down."

I notice her license plate when she slams the trunk shut. FNCY F33T. This gives me a chuckle. It's funny not because it's clever, but rather the stark contrast between the two of us. My minivan flaunts a decal in the rear window that reads: *Condoms prevent minivans*. We could *not* be more different.

Driving over the Jensen Beach Causeway this morning, the view is breathtaking. The Intracoastal water exposes varying shades of aqua. Fish jump, welcoming us as we drive along the bridge from Hutchinson Island to Jensen. The sky is clear and uninterrupted by clouds. It stretches endlessly, evoking a feeling of calm and tranquility. The sun rises above the sea, enhancing its beauty with its warmth and promise of a new day.

"Our little town is paradise. Right?" Gina squeals, momentarily taking her hands off the wheel, flailing her arms above her head. "Wheee!"

I am excited and terrified, but I'm enjoying every moment. Gina finds ways to bring joy to every day, and I'm thankful we're friends.

"I love the sunglasses. They match yours. We're twins."

"You can keep them." She smiles in my direction.

For a minute, I pretend we're sisters—an older, fun sister I never had. I'm reminded of a quote I love by Winnie-the-Pooh, "Today is my new favorite day."

We park in front of a cozy yellow bungalow slightly off Jensen Beach Boulevard.

"This is the Bunk House," Gina says, adjusting her windblown hair in the rearview mirror. "You're gonna love it here."

Just as we make our way up the walkway to the entrance, we're greeted by the owner.

"Hey Gina, good to see you."

"Hello Kelly, I brought my friend Holly with me today."

Kelly holds the door open for us to enter. Her enthusiasm is palpable. She suggests we try the freshly baked, gluten-free, vegan carrot cake cupcakes. I can't help but notice her long, silky brown hair—not one out of place, as I run my fingers through my hair-blown mess.

Gina orders cappuccinos for the two of us and two cupcakes. When they arrive, I'm impressed by the beauty of something as simple as a cupcake. You can almost feel the care put into this tiny creation. The cupcake dons cream cheese icing, and it's sprinkled with cinnamon. Almost too pretty to eat, I break apart a small piece, and my mouth thanks me with a smile I can't hold back.

After a few sips of coffee, Gina brings me up to speed on the other families in our cul-de-sac, less the Hudson sisters. No one knows them well. Those ladies keep to themselves.

Gina reaches inside the pocket of her leggings for a copy of the diagram she created for me, "Alright, Holly, here we go. Counterclockwise, right to left around the cul-de-sac, the first is Harry. Dirty Harry, actually, but not in a Clint Eastwood kind of way, rather because he references uncomfortable sexual innuendo to everything you say. His fourteen-year-old son, Chet, is also a bit peculiar."

"They live beside the dog park," I say.

"Yes. Then there's Harrington next door to Harry and Chet. Harrington is a stay-at-home dad who gave up his career in architecture to raise his two toddler daughters, Ana and Eva. His wife, Greta, works uncommon hours within the financial markets."

"I love that. Girl power, I'm going to like her."

"The Hudson house is next. The Hudsons were one of the original homeowners of Laguna Palms. Their father is a very well-respected judge in these parts. Let's move on."

"Why? I'd like to know more about them?"

"Nope. Not today."

"Living beside the sisters is Chloe." Gina continues, "She's a kindergarten special needs teacher who inherited the house from her aunt. Chloe is a true do-gooder. She donated a kidney to a student's mom. She's our local hero. Her husband, Fred, invented a foldable electric golf cart—a genius design that folds inward. The larger model's third-row seating folds to help fit the golf cart into smaller spaces like a one-car garage, taking up the same space as a golf cart with only two rows of seating. He used to be a firefighter, but once he retired, his invention made millions after selling the patent to a famous golf cart company, which will remain unnamed due to an ironclad nondisclosure agreement."

"Really?"

"Here's the irony," Gina says. "For an automobile designer, he's a terrible driver. He crashes into something nearly every week, so watch out for your kids."

"Duly noted," I nod.

Gina continues, "Their twelve-year-old daughter, Luna, is a delight. She's petite, blonde, friendly, full of random facts, and falls somewhere on the spectrum."

I must look overwhelmed by all this information because Gina rubs my shoulders and says, "Finally,

Patty lives next door to Chloe. She's the current HOA president—an older woman recovering from a small stroke she had a few months back, but watch out...she bites. She can make your stay here with us rather difficult with petty grievances, like a dirty walkway, smelly garbage cans, or misshapen hedges, etc. Keep a fair distance."

"I'm going to need a nap after all of that," I suggest, trying to be funny, but not really. It's a lot to remember.

After paying for breakfast and an assurance to Kelly to return soon, Gina promises, "Don't worry, Holly, I've got you. I'll watch out for you around here. You can count on me."

I'm not sure if she actually means that or if she's trying to be neighborly, but in that instant, I realized that as much as I love my family, having a good friend is something I didn't know I needed until now.

Later that afternoon, Gina introduces me to Charlie, the driver the residents hire to get around town. I immediately hire him to take my kids to and from school because why have money if you can't truly enjoy it? Having a driver to tote around those three little monsters is the most significant monetary perk, second only to Francesca, the cleaning lady and part-time nanny, who works weekdays, helping to keep my home and kids in order.

A week later, Patty suggests at the HOA meeting that we begin a fruitcake exchange for Christmas. I thought it was a dumb idea. But Gina, in her defense, suggests that it may be an excellent way to get to know the neighbors better, outside of morning pleasantries and casual greetings at the fitness center, country club, or quarterly HOA meetings.

Harrington, the stay-at-home dad, is the first to volunteer to bake and deliver a fruitcake on Christmas Eve. His family is from England, with ancestors from Wales. He will make a traditional English fruitcake, otherwise known as Christmas cake or plum cake. I never would have guessed that fruitcakes and their traditions vary so widely from country to country.

In English tradition, the fruitcake brings good tidings into the new year, and Harrington will be the first to bestow his good graces.

Chapter Five

The English Fruitcake
Christmas Eve 2018

The morning of December twenty-fourth starts off lovely. Birds sing, and squirrels frolic and climb the oaks and palm trees in the neighborhood.

"Good morning, girls. Rise and shine, my lovelies. Oh, Mr. Sun, Sun, Mr. Golden Sun, please shine down on me. Down, down, down on me," Harrington sings, embellishing the original lyrics with his best Barney impression.

Kids these days don't know who Barney & Friends are, but since *he* is home raising the girls, he gets to choose the morning lineup with some of his favorite entertainers from his childhood. The best function of smart TVs is that you can stream any show anytime without being confined to local TV times and annoying commercials.

"Today, I've got to get you girls off swiftly for your half-day preschool holiday party at the Children's Museum. I know how much you both love the museum. I'm going to bake two Christmas cakes before mom gets home this morning," he says in his most enthusiastic daddy voice.

"What's a Christmas cake?" Three-year-old Ana contorts her face in confusion.

"Well, it's a cake my grandparents made in England for the holidays. Maybe one day soon we can visit them. They are too old to travel here. Until then, you'll have to eat *my* cake. I'm no baker, but I'll try my best."

"Daddy, the last time you made brownies, they died."

"Burnt, not died, honey. I'll try harder this time around. I promise." He reminds himself, Bloom where you are planted, something his mom used to say. While he could build important structures for Florida's transportation needs at work, he's home raising the girls—for now—Bloom where you are planted. I'll try harder. I can do this, he thinks.

"Why two cakes, Daddy?"

"One for us and one for our neighbor, Patty. In England, you bake a cake for a neighbor to bring good luck into the new year."

"Does Patty *need* good luck?"

"We could *all* use some good luck, honey. Sit down, and I'll make you some French toast," he says. But two-year-old Eva shows up crying before he can smack butter into the frying pan.

"Eva, honey, what's wrong?"

"My throat hurts, Daddy."

"Okay, baby. Maybe you can stay home with me today and help Daddy bake the cakes."

"I want to stay home too," Ana chimes in.

"Well, it's Christmas Eve, so . . . sure, let's all stay home and bake the cakes."

"Yay!" the girls sing out, jumping with delight.

"Will Mommy help too?" asks Eva.

"I am not sure when she will be home this morning." Greta works in finance with pre-market futures. She works from 8:00 p.m. to 10:00 a.m. These hours are not usually set in stone. She has a few demanding clients that keep her in the office until noon on some days.

Harrington manages through breakfast, the French toast of champions he calls it, then watches a bit of *Barney & Friends* and *PAW Patrol* with the girls before he starts baking. He takes out the Lego bricks for the girls to play with in the kitchen to entertain them while he bakes.

"We want to help, Daddy," says little Eva.

"You two can help me stir the batter in the bowl when I'm ready."

"Okay, Daddy."

He opens the Lego fire station, and they sit on the kitchen rug and empty the Lego bricks from the box. His wife, Greta, would have loved him to spend more time reading with the girls, but he prefers teaching them to construct and build. He believes that math and logic are the cornerstones of intelligence.

Harrington prepares the batter. Ana asks for a drink as he folds the cherries, citrus peel, apples, walnuts, and pecans into the cake batter. Turning toward the refrigerator, he knocks the mixing bowl off the counter onto the floor. Luckily, the batter did not spill or splatter.

He grabs two cups from the cabinet and pours lemonade into them because what one of them wants, the other will undoubtedly want as well. When the doorbell rings, he places the cups on the kids' table in the nook. Harrington rushes over to open the door for Charlie.

"Hello, Mr. Barnes. Are the girls ready for the Christmas celebration at the museum?"

"Oh crap, Charlie, I forgot to call you. They will not be going. Eva is not feeling well, and um, it's a holiday and all, you know. I'm sorry."

"That's quite alright, Mr. Barnes. No worries. Have a merry Christmas."

"Charlie, before you go, my wife bought you a gift. Let me go get it."

Harrington races to the kitchen counter to grab the gift for Charlie and notices the girls fighting over who gets to stir the batter next.

"My turn now," Eva yells.

"Hey, girls, that's enough fun in the kitchen. Back to building." He snatches the wooden spoon and bowl and returns the kids to the carpet with the Lego bricks. He hands the gift to Charlie and wishes him a merry Christmas.

When Greta arrives shortly after 10:00 a.m., Harrington and the girls are fast asleep on the couch. Elmo is singing to his goldfish friend, Dorothy, on the TV. She quietly makes her way to the bedroom to sneak in a nap as well before the kids wake up.

At 11:30 a.m., with the cakes cooling on the counter in the kitchen, Harrington wakes up first. He enters the bedroom to kiss his wife and welcome her home.

"What are the girls doing at home?"

"Eva is not feeling well, so I had them both stay home and help me bake the Christmas cakes."

"You would never know it. The kitchen is spotless."

"You know me—Mr. Clean."

"Yup, and the bald head and muscles to prove it," she says, kissing him while rubbing his shiny, perfectly round head.

"MOM, MOM!" Eva cries out, and they scurry into the living room to see what is happening. "There's someone at the door," Eva says, pointing toward the entrance.

Harrington opens the door. It's Patty.

"Hello, Harrington. I just dropped by to collect the fruitcake, if it's ready. I know you're very busy with the girls, and I also wanted to see them."

The two girls run over and hug Patty. She brings candy or coloring books every time she visits, so they love her. Kids can very easily be bought.

"Look what I have here, girls. Christmas coloring books, just for you two."

"What do you say, girls?" pleads Greta.

"Thank you," they both chime in.

"You didn't have to come here. I would have delivered it this afternoon," says Harrington.

"It was no bother."

"Merry Christmas," he offers as he hands Patty the Christmas cake decorated nicely with vanilla icing and dusted with confectionary sugar. "Enjoy it. It's my family's recipe from England. Good tidings, Patty!"

"Good tidings, my friends," she says as she walks out the front door. The girls return to building, and Harrington suggests they clean up the Lego pieces and put them back in the box.

"I can't find the Dalmatian doggie," says Ana in a panic.

"It's got to be somewhere. It will show up," Harrington promises in his most optimistic voice.

At 11:00 p.m., an emergency rescue team arrives at Patty's house. The neighbors—every one of them except the Hudsons—are outside in the cul-de-sac, all worried about Patty. She had a stroke last year and has just begun to feel herself again. After fifteen minutes or so, the EMTs wheel her out on a gurney, a sheet covering her body.

"What happened?" Greta asks in despair as other neighbors ask in unison the same question repeatedly. Neither of the medics responded.

Fred, a former firefighter from Hutchinson Island's Station 14, approaches the rescue team. In the distance, Greta moves closer and can barely hear one mutter, "I think she choked on fruitcake."

"We pulled this out of her throat," the other continues. He shows Fred a large walnut and the tiny Lego Dalmatian dog captured in a ziplock bag. "These must have gotten lodged in her throat," he adds. "She called the police, hardly able to speak. She must have tried to leave the house to get help. We found her lying by the front door. Unfortunately, we were too late to save her." Under his breath, looking sullen, he quietly continues, "The cons of living alone."

"Oh dear God," and "Oh heavens," misty-eyed neighbors cry as the gurney carrying Patty is placed in the back of the ambulance.

There it is, in the hands of one medic, staring back at Greta and Harrington—the miniature doggie Ana was looking for.

Through a cloud of tears, Greta whispers to her husband, "So sad. So sorry this happened to her." Both Greta and Harrington are visibly shaken. Greta sinks her head into her hands, tears spilling.

Harrington embraces Greta's petite frame with his large shoulders and says, "We must never tell the girls about this."

Greta agrees. "Of course not. It was obviously an accident."

"This morning, when I left the kitchen to answer the door," Harrington explains, "Charlie showed up to take the girls to school. They must have dropped the Lego into the mixture when I walked away."

This was a dramatic ending to our first cake gifting, but you would be mistaken if you thought it would be the end of the Laguna Palms fruitcake exchange. Sadly, this was just the first untimely death by fruitcake.

Chapter Six

Trapped
December 2, 2022
The Captive

I awake, hoping all of this is just some lucid dream. Ouch! Pain emanates from my right leg, now chained to the damp gray concrete wall.

A cold feeling washes over me. I'm frightened. I'm shaking. My head feels heavy. The stubble on my face is itchy. My tongue is swollen. It seems too big for my mouth. A dull hum fills my ears. I look around the small, eerie space, trying to figure out what has happened and if I'll be able to escape. Everywhere I turn, there is emptiness. I squint in the darkness. I can make out only a bed in the corner, far smaller than I've ever seen.

My worst fears are confirmed as I come to the realization that I've been kidnapped and am now being held captive in this basement. The moment that door slammed shut yesterday, my reality splintered in two: my old life and the current hell in which I find myself. Panic grips me, and I feel like I will drift off once again as tears stream down my face. I sink into a corner of the room, not knowing what will come next.

As I sit here in the basement, my mind racing, there is no escape in sight. What will happen to me now? I push these thoughts away and focus on a small ray of hope that someone will find me. I refuse to give up. I must find a way out of this.

But in the meantime, I am stuck in this unfamiliar place, and there is nothing I can do but wait. My sense of uneasiness intensifies. I groan in frustration, then bite down on my lower lip, a bad habit over which I have limited control. I bite too hard. My mouth fills with blood, a familiar copper taste. This brings me comfort, however, in a strange, twisted way.

"Hellllp!" I shout as loud as I'm able. I'm not stupid. I've watched enough horror movies to know that if someone takes the time and effort to capture a person, chances are they took the time to make sure sound can't penetrate. I try anyway.

"Help! Help!" I shout louder, desperate now. My watch shows a ten percent battery charge. Surely, people have noticed that I'm missing.

"Hello? Someone help me! My ankle hurts! I'm hungry! I need to pee!" No answer. "Why am I here?"

Suddenly, from a speaker above that I could not find: "You know why you're here!"

"Fuck, fuck, fuck me. Just kill me now!"

Chapter Seven

Pilates
January 2019
Holly

You can tell a lot about a person in an exercise class. Aggression, stamina, determination, endurance, feelings of self-worth, and pain tolerance are all on full display for everyone to see. You can't hide your true self during intense physical activity.

Today, I accompany Gina to a Pilates class in Stuart. I'm excited to make new friends. Physical suffering binds people in a way that everyday life can't. You know exactly what I mean if you've ever been part of a sports team or regular Spin, aerobics, or Pilates class.

When we arrive in the parking lot, I playfully tell Gina, "I hope Pilates works for me. I went to the paint store to get thinner. It didn't work."

"You're funny, Holly."

"Not really. I heard some comedian tell that joke before. It's not an original."

Gina pulls open the large glass entrance door to the studio and announces, "Hello, everyone. This is my new friend, Holly." That earns us broad smiles and a few waves from a group of ladies with sculpted bodies and overly injected lips.

"I come as often as possible," Gina says, grabbing my hand and dragging me into the locker room. "Pilates is a great workout for the body and soul."

"It's also great to keep in shape for extra-curricular activities," a much older woman says with a wink as they enter the locker room.

"Holly, this is Millie. She's fabulous. She's in her seventies and comes nearly every day to the eleven o'clock class."

Millie nods and takes a sip from her water bottle that reads Might Be Water, Might Be Vodka, which gives me a little chuckle.

"I walk three miles with friends most mornings out on Jensen Beach, but try to make the eleven a.m. Pilates class at least three times a week," Millie explains. "Gotta keep your body strong for the young men these days," she says while touching her toes, then stretching side to side and backward, showing off her not-so-seventies body.

I feel myself blush, suddenly flustered. Then I laugh. "I want to be you when I grow up," I say while trying to stretch. I'm barely able to reach past my knees, never mind touch my toes. I take the scrunchy from my wrist and pull my unruly black hair into a ponytail.

Gina drops her overpriced pink Ferragamo bag into a locker before class begins. I also have a few designer bags, but mine are bought "pre-loved" from Poshmark, while I'm sure hers are preordered for each new season.

Class begins, and we start with a stretch. A bevy of long-legged blondes watch themselves in the mirror, puckering their lips and ensuring every hair is in place. Ridiculous, I think. It's an exercise class, not a fashion show. Then I catch myself. Everything is a fashion show. I put a pin in that for my brain to process—a note-to-self, so to speak. Everything is a fashion show!

"Holly, I was thinking," Gina suggests, "you should start a mommy blog. I mean, your husband is off doing God-knows-what three weeks out of every month, and when the kids are off at school, you should do something for yourself, even if you don't need the money. I bet lots of moms would love to read about what it's like raising triplets."

"I'm no do-gooder mommy blogger—more of a sarcastic, mean girl, to be honest. A 'just let me get through the day without verbally harming anyone, including my kids' kind of mom."

"You are *so* not a mean girl, Holly, and let's just put aside what you say about your kids. I know you love them."

"I mean, my thoughts are definitely mean girl. You don't live in my head. On the outside, let's just say . . . I pretend pretty well."

Gina, startled, inhales deeply, then asks, "Really? Okay, mean girl, what was your first impression of me?"

"Alright . . . let's see. My mean girl mind said, 'Watch out. Just like in nature, the most colorful creatures are venomous.' Also, 'OMG, she's fucking huge,' comes to mind as well."

She bores her eyes into me; a few seconds pass, then she laughs out loud. "That's hilarious."

"And then when you talked about being a foot fetish mod—"

Gina cuts me off, her hand gesturing for me to stop. "Okay, mean girl, that's enough for now. Back to sweet Holly, the great pretender, please."

When class ends, I feel sore in a way that I know walking downstairs will be an issue. My quads and hamstrings are already screaming.

"Let's go to lunch," suggests Gina.

"Sure. I have a few more hours before the kids get home," I say while collecting my towel and water bottle.

Millie changes from her sneakers to platform wedges. The wedges are higher than I would ever dare try.

"Nice meeting you and I hope to see you again soon," Millie yells out as she rushes past us on her way out of the studio.

"That woman is a beast," I mutter as the door slams shut.

"You don't know the half of it. She knows everyone in town, and I mean everyone in Hutchinson, Jensen Beach, and Stuart. The mayor, the sheriff, every criminal . . ."

"I'm sorry, I thought that was you."

"Nope, I got nothin' on *that* lady. She's the queen of the treasure coast."

On the drive back home, we take a detour through Jensen Beach to enjoy the scenery of the intercostal, old Florida homes and boutique motels just before the Jensen Beach Causeway, bringing us back to the island.

"STOP, STOP, STOP," Gina yells as we drive past a hotdog stand on the side of the road. "Turn around. Let's go *there* for lunch." She points to the bright blue outdoor mobile kitchen with a colorfully painted dancing hamburger and hotdog. "You're going to love Fredgie's World Famous Hot Dogs!"

"Hello, Toni," Gina squeals in excitement as soon as the passenger side door of my minivan slams shut.

"Welcome back, Gina," Toni says. "What can I get for you today?"

"Today, I would like the Fredgie Original."

"What's that?" I ask curiously. Hotdogs for lunch? I guess as long as her feet stay in shape, all is well.

"An award-winning hotdog with peanut butter, chili, and spicy mustard," explains Toni.

Sounds disgusting, I think, but I fear to say it aloud. All that work and pain in Pilates, and we end up here? On the side of the road in Jensen, surrounded by seagulls and squirrels begging for scraps?

"Two, please," orders Gina, removing a twice-folded twenty-dollar bill from a small pocket hidden within her sports bra.

I can't quite explain it: this tangy, spicy, sweet carnival snack of culinary delight. To be honest, it may have been one of the most delicious meals I ever had.

Chapter Eight

The Prison Jumpsuit
December 3, 2022
The Captive

T oday, I wake in a tiny bed, my feet dangling. My mouth is dry as sand, ankle seething in pain. My clothes have been removed and replaced with . . . what am I wearing? Orange scrubs? If it wasn't clear that I was a prisoner before, it's crystal clear now. The pants snap between my legs. Must be for ease of removing them due to my ankle bracelet. Another set of orange scrubs is folded nicely by the bed. I hold up the shirt. On the back is a prison number: 34996. Only that's not a number you would find in the prison system in Florida. That's our zip code!

I hear church music or a choir . . . gospel? I can't tell. "Ave Maria," "Amazing Grace," "Go Tell It on the Mountain," "Bridge over Troubled Water," then "Shackles" by Mary Mary, and the irony is not lost on me. Someone has a warped sense of humor.

The metal door creaks open, and a meatball sub, a small metal bowl full of Ruffles potato chips, and a two-liter bottle of Sprite lying on its side slide slowly toward me on a tray.

The gray metal tray disappears every evening as I sleep and returns the next day. A washbasin full of water, a towel, a bar of Ivory soap, and an orange Home Depot bucket where I relieve myself are also removed and replaced every evening with just the right amount of toilet paper. I mark the wall by scraping my fingernail every morning when I wake, just like unfortunate prisoners in movies.

My stomach churns and growls—my mouth waters at the sight of food. I'm starving. When I reach for the meatball sub, I notice an envelope in the center of the tray, lying against the two-liter bottle of Sprite. I don't want to read it. I'm afraid of what it might say.

Light illuminates the dark dungeon through a tiny rectangular window, just out of reach, when a crack of thunder roars, shudders, and shakes the house. Rain pelts heavily against the window. Suddenly, I can smell the rain. The scent of fresh air and autumn leaves hits my senses. I can't actually smell the rain, but my mind comforts me with a familiar scent to soothe my soul.

The window is familiar. I've seen it before, along my morning walking path. The house on the hill in the cul-de-sac. It's the only house in the community with a basement window. I know where I am now. Everyone in the neighborhood knows about this place.

The Hudson house.

Chapter Nine

Judge Hudson
March 2023

A judge doesn't simply preside over hearings and resolve disputes. He or she also utilizes their critical thinking and decision-making skills to apply the law without bias to punish or reward opposing parties for the betterment of society. But, in a nutshell, a judge's underlying goal is often to right a specific wrong to create a better community for all involved. While no one can play God—other than God, of course—a judge is the next great powerful resource.

All AJ Hudson ever wanted to be was . . . remembered. Remembered when he's gone for leaving this world a better place than he found it. Remembered for a life of service to a community that he loved. He believed every decision he ever made was for the greater good. Early in his law career, he decided to take on the burden of sacrificing the few for the betterment of the many.

His obituary says so little about the person he really was. An obituary . . . a random word salad of facts. He may have been better understood had he written his own. Many townsfolk wished he had.

Judge Alexander James (AJ) Hudson
1952–2023

Judge Alexander James Hudson, 71, of Laguna Palms, Hutchinson Island, Florida, died from heart failure on March 15, 2023, in the emergency room at the Cleveland Clinic.

Judge Hudson was born on July 4, 1952, to Frank and Clara Hudson, English immigrants. He was an only child. He was predeceased by his wife, Esther, and two children, Trudy and Leigh. Judge Hudson and his wife, Esther, had fostered eleven children, many of whom have since become prominent figures in South Florida.

Judge Hudson graduated from college and later obtained his Juris Doctor at the University of Florida in 1982, after serving in Vietnam from 1971 until the war ended in April 1975.

Judge Hudson worked as a public defender for ten years, then ascended to the judiciary in 1993, serving as a circuit judge on the 19th Judicial District in both juvenile and family court, where he worked until his death.

A public servant and pillar of the community for all his life, Judge Hudson was recognized for his distinguished judicial career and civic-mindedness. Among his family, he was remembered for his warmth and generosity, wisdom, and steadfast moral code.

His extended foster family kindly asks for donations to the Hibiscus Children's Center in Jensen Beach to continue Judge Hudson's passion for the care and well-being of children within the community.

It's a word salad of facts no one really cared about that tells you very little about the man he was and his intentions for better tomorrows for the local community that he and the four generations of Hudsons before him have called home.

What you wouldn't know from the obituary was that AJ never sent a minor off to jail or the juvenile detention center. He offered *every* juvenile defendant who appeared before him in court a second chance, sometimes three or four. The lucky ones he fostered in his own home. Those fortunate few have gone on to become prominent figures in the community: police officers, councilmen and women, doctors, nurses, and teachers.

AJ and his family found ways to bring out the best, but also reign in the worst tendencies of each individual. He believed that everyone has both good and bad proclivities. The goal was always the ability to control them and use them for the greater good. For example, one of the teens brought before the court for stockpiling explosives in his garage was offered a lucrative career in the Office of Emergency Management & Homeland Security Bomb Squad Unit—thanks to Judge Hudson.

However, due to an unfortunate string of events that Judge Hudson may or may not have been aware of, some in this town will forever remember this man as the one person responsible for bringing evil to Laguna Palms.

Chapter Ten

Super Bowl Party
February 3, 2019
Holly

There is something about a neighborhood party that brings a community together. Sharing junk food and cocktails, common gripes about HOA fees, traffic caused by snowbirds, new construction tearing up native preserves, recommendations for new restaurants, and gossip about weird neighbors somehow brings people closer. Shared experiences amongst friends bring about some of the most joyful moments in life.

Every neighborhood has at least one signature annual outing or party. For our small circle within Laguna Palms, it's the Super Bowl. Chloe and Fred host a Super Bowl party every year. Fred is a huge football fan. This year, all seven families in the cul-de-sac were invited. Well, five, actually. No one has moved into Patty's house since she passed, and everyone stays clear of the Hudson sisters.

Rams versus Patriots. A party on a Sunday, entertaining commercials, a fun halftime show featuring Adam Levine of Maroon 5, and multiple glimpses of a sweaty Tom Brady? You don't need to ask twice.

Bradley and I are the first to arrive. Chloe's house looks so inviting from the street. Light blue with yellow shutters, it looks like a home in a fairy tale. She has a slew of gnomes hidden between purple periwinkle plants surrounding her oak tree in the front yard. One pesky gnome tries to scale the tree with a rope while another lady gnome she calls Petunia walks a ladybug on a leash. A larger gnome with a happy little grin holds a taco in each hand. He's my favorite. Being from Miami, I'm more of a fancy, pink flamingo staked-on-the-lawn kind of gal— but to each their own.

Walking along the driveway, we see Fred whizzing around the cul-de-sac in his bright red golf cart prototype, his daughter, Luna, squealing in delight. Then we hear a loud crash. I whirl around and meet Fred's eyes. He quietly screams, "Shit, shit," then a much louder, "SHIT!"

"Fred . . . Luna, are you two alright?" I ask. He seems fine, but the mailbox—not so much. It's hanging from its post, barely able to hang on.

"Don't tell Chloe. I'll fix it before she knows it's been injured."

"Never saw a thing," says Bradley, shaking his head, and then places the hanging mailbox back upon its post. "There ya go. No harm, no foul."

We enter with Fred and Luna trailing behind after Luna grabs a tray of chicken wings from her dad's truck. All four of us are in matching Brady football jerseys. Fred hugs my husband ferociously, then pats him on the back as we walk over the threshold. "Thanks for coming, bro, and for helping out. Glad you're in town for this."

Luna immediately distracts her mom, Chloe, with some game day facts while Fred texts Harley, the neighborhood handyman. Luna looks much like her mom, except for a few tiny freckles on her nose and cheeks.

"Mom," says Luna with a nervous smile, "did you know that 100 million people are estimated to be watching the Super Bowl today? That's almost one-third of the entire US population. Also, the Super Bowl is in Atlanta this year, but Miami has hosted it more than any other city since its inception in 1967."

"Is that right?" asks Chloe, feigning interest and looking past her to get a glimpse of what Fred is up to.

"Yes, Mom . . . are you listening to me?"

Watching Chloe with Luna makes me laugh because everyone knows ninety-five percent of parenting is feigning interest in what your kids are saying.

"Yes, I hear you, Luna. Anything else?"

"Yes. Dad and I picked up some buffalo chicken wings from Shuckers since this is the most popular Super Bowl snack. Dad thinks Shuckers wings are the best on the island." She hands the platter to her mom and sits down on the couch. In the meantime, Fred is still texting Harley.

> Help! in dire need of a favor. Just smashed into [mailbox emoji] It's in poor condition. What are the chances you can fix this tonight before Chloe notices? [praying hands emoji]

I peek over Fred's shoulder and notice the ellipsis. Harley is typing back.

> I'm with family getting ready to watch the big game. [football emoji] Can't this wait until tomorrow?

Fred frantically types back with multiple dollar sign emojis.

> There is an extra $100 in it for you if you can do this during the half-time show

Harley writes back with a hammer emoji.

> I'll be there

Fred fires off a final message.

> Also, bring white paint, the post is pretty scraped up.

When Harrington and Greta arrive with the kids, Luna brings them straightaway into the kids' movie theater to watch *Shrek*. The home Chloe inherited from her aunt has miniature leather movie theatre seating for twelve children. Plus, she has it decked out with a popcorn machine and a refrigerator filled with Fiji water and blue Gatorade.

"We should have brought our kids, too," Bradley whispers in my ear.

"I'm sure that you're kidding. We can't unleash our gremlins on these poor people. We are trying to *make* friends, remember? They are better off at home with Francesca."

"Right, of course," he says, but what would *he* know? He's never around. He thinks the kids are delightful. He only sees them at their best. Also, he arrives with presents upon every return. So they adore him.

"Where is Gina tonight?" I ask.

"She has to work. An important client needed her on a Zoom call." Chloe winks.

"Gotcha," I say.

We join Harrington and Greta as they pour themselves a glass of merlot in the kitchen.

"Holly, I've been meaning to talk to you. We should get our kids together for a playdate soon, since they're so close in age," Greta suggests, then takes a small sip of wine. She looks so sincere. Her big brown eyes, giant eyeglasses, and short bob haircut make her look so much like Velma from *Scooby-Doo*—intelligent, quick-witted. Wouldn't she know better than to ask about a playdate with my three bandits?

"I'm not sure you really want to do that. I have triplet three-year-olds—well, four in two weeks. I can barely keep up with them, even with my housekeeper and our driver helping on most days."

"Well, I was thinking maybe just take them for a trip to the park. You know, some fresh air and exercise? Or a walk along the beach and play in the sand after school."

"Sure. Let's plan a playdate soon. I'll mark it on the calendar for when they turn eight."

"Funny," she says with a smile after another sip of wine. "I'm serious, Holly. There are so few kids on the island. Our kids should be friends."

"Okay, okay." I nod. "We can talk about it later."

A few moments later, Dirty Harry bursts through the front door. "Hey, what happened to your mailbox?"

"What?" asks Chloe.

Fred grabs Harry by the elbow and ushers him away to explain the situation, and I say, "Chloe, can I ask you about the vegetable dip? I was hoping to get the recipe from you." I have learned that if you ask Chloe about food, recipes, or specialty dishes, she will pivot away from anything to talk about anything culinary. Whoosh, close call.

I'm beginning to sweat a little. I tap my middle finger and thumb together ten times with my right hand. Sounds silly, I know, but it helps me in anxious situations. I picked this up in third grade from a boy named Justin. At first, I wondered why he did this when the teacher called on him, but after trying it myself, I fully understood.

Chloe goes on and on about all the different vegetables she cut up: celery, scallions, carrots, et cetera, added sour cream and seasonings, yada yada. My mind trails off. Motherhood has ruined my attention span.

Chloe continues, "Cool the dip in the fridge for two hours . . ."

Instead of the recipe, I focus on her. She's so sweet and looks adorable today, her long blonde hair in a ponytail, the Brady jersey fitting her like a dress, engulfing her tiny five-foot frame.

Across the room, Harry is getting an earful from Fred. I vaguely overheard him say, "She'll kill me if she finds out . . ." and ". . . getting it fixed today."

"Where is Chet tonight, Harry?" Bradley asks from across the living room.

"He's got a movie date with a freshman girl at school." I'm shocked, and I'm sure that's not true. I can't imagine any sane girl with the slightest bit of self-respect would date that little weirdo.

"And what on God's green earth are you wearing, Harry? Look around. You are the only Rams fan," Chloe points out.

"Yup, I'm pulling for the underdog," he says proudly. "Brady can't win *every* year."

"We'll see about that! Greatest of all time, you know! I can't wait for the big game to start," Fred says, rubbing his hands together in excitement. "Big score. It's gonna be big, so big."

"That's what she said," Harry chimes in. No one laughs except Fred and Bradley.

Harry is so predictable, immature, and annoying. All of the guys are, actually. I think Fred intentionally sets Dirty Harry up for his disturbing hot takes. The two of them are peas in a pod. Harry and Fred look like they could be brothers. Thick, curly brown hair, hockey player build—less all the missing teeth—broad-shouldered, husky. They stand maybe six foot one or so. They both have dad-bod bellies. My unscientific theory about dad-bods is that they often gain weight when their wives are pregnant. I think the appropriate term is coined sympathy weight. But for some dads, they don't lose it. Those two are also crazy football fans and workaholics. Fred is a retired firefighter and now an esteemed golf cart/auto designer.

On the other hand, Harry graduated from Cornell with gentlemen's Cs. He learned more about hazing, beer pong, and every type of flavored vodka than organic chem or finance. He has a thriving business, nevertheless, specializing in acquisitions. He buys up companies and tears them apart for profit.

Before the game begins, Chloe says, "Hey, everyone, can we make a toast? Everyone, please raise your glass." We all meet in the kitchen in a small circle like a huddle before a high school football game.

"Thank you all for coming. Fred and I are thankful for your friendship. Let's remember that we are missing one of our own today. To Patty. You will be missed and forever in our hearts."

We all clink glasses. Greta's face reddens, and Harrington walks out to the pool deck for a moment. Greta and Harrington are obviously still very upset about Patty's death.

The game begins, Brady gets the ball, and the announcer says, "Brady is desperately looking to score tonight."

"Me too," says Harry. "Me too." He can be so gross.

After the first quarter, the game is scoreless and, I dare say, extremely boring. Luna brings Ana and Eva out of the movie room for a snack and says, "Hey, did you know that the Super Bowl is the second-biggest eating day of the year, behind Thanksgiving?" She piles four chicken wings, Mexican dip with Tostitos, and a lasagna square onto her plate.

"Don't overeat, Luna," says Chloe. "Too much gluten can make your stomach upset."

"Don't *drink* too much, Mom," Luna quips back snidely. "Alcohol can make your kidney upset. Remember, you only have one."

"Touché," says Chloe with a nod. "I'll be good. I promise."

Ana pulls at Greta's jersey and says, "Look, Mommy, I made a pretty puzzle."

"Let me see," says Greta. "A Rubik's Cube. Did you complete this all by yourself?"

"It's Luna's toy. She helped me. Can I have one?"

"Sure, Ana. I know how much you love puzzles."

"Just like you, Mommy."

"Alright then. Maybe for your birthday?"

"Okay, Mommy," she says, then runs off, leaving Greta with the Rubik's Cube.

As I walk out front to catch a break from football talk and stupid sexual football innuendo, Harley pulls up—another one in a Brady jersey.

"I thought you were coming at halftime?"

"Well, boring game and Fred seems pretty distraught."

"Definitely," I say. "I saw the praying hands emoji. He's desperate."

"Looks like an easy fix. It just popped off the post. I can nail it back in place in a jiffy and touch up the post with some paint."

"Good luck," I say. "I'll tell him you fixed it."

I walk back inside as Greta hands the Rubik's Cube to Chloe.

"I think this is Luna's."

"Actually, it's mine," says Chloe. "It's an original from the eighties. My aunt gave it to me. I have a whole collection in the game room: this three-by-three original, a four-by-four, one that's egg-shaped, a triangle-shaped one, and an octahedron."

"Ana loves it. I'll have to buy her one for her birthday. We just love puzzles."

Halftime delights us ladies with a shirtless Adam Levine and guest appearances from Travis Scott and Big Boi. The men hardly pay any attention. They're upset about such a low-scoring game. Three to zero, finally a score after a forty-two-yard field goal for New England. Geez.

When the second half resumes, the commentator says, again about Brady, "The way he can stuff that ball into such tight spaces is amazing." We all brace for a comment from Dirty Harry, but none comes. He's gone.

"Where the heck is Harry?" Fred asks, agitated, turning his Patriots hat around, bill toward the back.

"No idea. Must have gone home," suggests Bradley with a shrug.

"That's not like him to just up and leave like that without saying goodbye. The Irish goodbye is out of character for him. He's usually the last to leave." Fred stands and begins to pace around the room. The rest of us watch him without saying a word. A few minutes pass before Fred says, "I'll call him on his cell . . . three rings, then straight to voicemail. I'm calling Chet."

"No, don't alarm the kid. That's not necessary. Holly and I will check in on him after the game," says Bradley. I roll my eyes.

Maybe he got a text from some lady he met on Bumble or Tinder, or whatever weird single men use these days to meet desperate women, I thought. However unlikely that may be. What I actually said was, "Maybe he got a text to hook up with a lady friend?"

"Maybe," Fred says flatly. "I don't know. Something feels off about his sudden departure."

He scratches at his neck. Red welts begin to appear. He's very worried about his friend.

After the game, Bradley and I walk across the circle toward Harry's house and notice a black SUV parked in the driveway of the Hudson house. Strange. No license plate. When we arrive at Harry's house, we knock, then ring Harry's bell. The bell is stuck. It doesn't ring.

"Push it in harder this time," says Bradley. I can't help but burst out in laughter.

"Push it in harder this time? Go ahead, say it!"

We both say in unison, "That's what she said."

The doorbell finally chimes, but no one answers.

"That's strange," Bradley says. "Maybe he did race off to be with some lady friend."

"Lady friend, that's funny."

"Don't be so judgmental. There is someone out there for everyone."

"I guess."

"Let's try again tomorrow. We'll come in the morning."

We catch each other's eyes and smirk this time, then repeat in unison, "Come in the morning." Hee-hee.

Chapter Eleven

The Letter
December 5, 2022
The Captive

My watch is dead. It's been dead for days now. I take it off. It's useless. Suddenly, time seems pointless. Like a child, I pretend to be pushed through a door to another realm where time stands still. I'm trapped, but soon I'll be saved. But who would save me? No one is my answer. This reality saddens me.

It's been two days since the letter was delivered. I can't bring myself to open it. They expect me to, and I feel empowered by the situation by refusing to read it. I win if I don't comply with their demands, right? My rebellious behavior is probably futile. Whatever hides within that envelope can be uncovered in other ways.

For forty-eight hours, I have had nothing to do but sit and stew in my thoughts in such deplorable conditions. The boredom is excruciating. I recreate happy childhood memories. I list songs I love in my head. I assemble a list of my absolute favorite horror movies. I start with *The Shining*, a classic, then add *The Exorcist*, *The Omen*, *Carrie*, and *Child's Play* because who doesn't love Chucky? I add *A Nightmare on Elm Street*, the *Scream* movies, *Insidious*, *The Haunting in Connecticut*, *The Cabin in the Woods*, *The Purge*, *The Ring*, *The Evil Dead*, *It*, *Hereditary*, *Halloween*, *Friday the 13th*, *Slender Man*, *Candyman*, *The Visit*, and the *Saw* movies, which are sick and twisted in all the ways I like. I go on and on. I ruminate about the genius of the indie film *The Babadook* for a moment, and finally, I end up with *Get Out*, which becomes my mantra and my goal…. *Get out*. I promise that when I get out of here, I'll obsess over a different genre—no more horror movies for me.

I finally conjure up the nerve to read the letter. *The Conjuring*. I add it to my favorite horror films. Time to face my predicament. The letter reads:

> *Please look toward the north wall and place your hand over the metal plate.*

I get up and do just that. A hologram appears. So real. I knew society would surely go in this direction, that someday we would attend concerts from bands and long-dead entertainers. Still, I never thought this technology would be ready for the consumer today. Wow. I blink a few times and rub my eyes. This is real. Surreal, actually.

A beautiful woman in a white cloak comes into view. She looks so real. She hovers about a foot off the floor like a ghost. She is staring directly at me. She blinks and smiles. The luminescent white cloak flows as if the wind controls her movement. A small piece of her hair falls from the cloak and sways, dancing with the imaginary wind. She's beautiful and terrifying at the same time.

"Welcome," she says, gesturing with her arms open wide. "We hope you are enjoying your stay with us in the Laguna Palms Rehabilitation Penitentiary. Our goal is to rehabilitate lost souls like yourself within our community. Think of this experience as a sort of born-again revitalization. Not in a Christian way, but rather as a form of redemption and revenge for those you have injured."

Suddenly, I feel cold. A blast of arctic air hits me. I look up at the vent positioned directly above me. I move away slightly, but it doesn't help. I shiver.

The hologram continues to speak. "You must master all five stages of penance to reacclimate back into society. Think of this like the step program in Alcoholics Anonymous. This process can take a few days or months, so the sooner you embrace your current situation and accept it, the sooner we can start on the road to redemption.

Only you can facilitate change in your life. You must change your current state of living. We offer you the opportunity to rewrite your narrative—and set your life's path in a new direction. You have been chosen. This is a gift. Embrace it!"

A gift? What the hell is going on? I wish this were just a prank, but I know it's not. I know what I've done.

"People always search for a simple solution for their complicated problems. It's easier to have faith in what you can't see versus doing the work in your life to make real change possible. We have already given you a few days of reflection, and tomorrow, we can start the work necessary to get you back to your normal life and the people you love most. It's important to understand that you can't move forward until you reckon with the past." The hologram flickers and continues.

"Please read the five-step plan. Follow along with the written letter in your possession."

I read along as she narrates.

"Number one, once prompted, you will admit ALL of your misgivings. Number two, you will ask for forgiveness, in writing, from all those you harmed. Number three, pray and reflect upon your atrocities, depending upon your religious or spiritual beliefs. Number four, punishment will be determined by the board of directors. Number five, redemption and release will be offered only after signing a nondisclosure agreement, which will be tied to the value of your home here in Laguna Palms. Should you break your promise of secrecy, we will take ownership of your home. In the aftermath, you will be allowed to pay it forward."

My teeth begin to chatter. I hug myself for warmth. I could grab the blanket from my bed but am too frightened to move. I focus on everything she says but have difficulty fully comprehending. This is a lot to take in.

The hologram flickers once again, returning with an eerie smile. I can't help but think this would be a great scene in a horror movie. The hologram, with its flickering effect and creepy smile. The woman's beauty. The cool air. It's disconcerting how the mind can trail off independently, even in dire situations. I pull myself back.

She continues, "Please remember that a body is temporary for the soul it encases. Treat your soul with the love and care it deserves, and be rewarded immediately in the afterlife and for all eternity."

I have no idea what the hell that means.

"To ease your worried mind, many men—and a few women—in your situation have been here in this basement, but only a few have perished."

Smoke fills the room from the vent above, and she disappears. Smoke . . . another excellent effect for a horror movie. Stop that! I scream inside my head. I have no words in response to this hologram and letter. I'm left stunned. Other men? Board of directors? What the hell? Is this some freakish cult?

I force my thoughts to reflect upon the quickest way to get out of here unharmed. Shall I search for something in this room I can use for a weapon or continue to scream, hoping anyone will hear me? Ultimately, I decide to do exactly as they ask, no matter the cost, so I could return home. Tears fall. I can't stop them. I squeeze my eyes shut in anger and scream silently.

Chapter Twelve

Meeting Esther
August 1982
Judge Hudson

A crowd gathered around a small girl, big brown eyes filled with tears, sitting on the bench at the bus stop one early summer morning. The girl, thin, sullen, tired, and hungry, sat in despair. Her two long braids were falling apart and frayed at the tips. She wore a tattered blue prairie dress. She had ended up here after traveling on many buses from Utah, escaping from her family's wishes for her to wed a man thirty years her senior.

She arrived with only a small suitcase, a rag doll her father gifted her as a small child, and eleven dollars in her pocket she had stolen from her mom's kitchen coffee tin hidden beneath the sink. This was the end of the line, the last stop on her final bus route. Feeling hopeless, she cried softly to herself because she had nowhere to go.

AJ Hudson pushed through a few nosy neighborhood ladies to introduce himself just as Luke, the chief of police, arrived at the scene. AJ heard the police car door slam behind him as he approached the girl on the bench.

"Hello. My name is AJ. AJ Hudson." He extended his hand to her, but she lowered her eyes and placed her hands on her lap, right hand over left.

"I just graduated from law school. I don't have much. I'm just an ordinary guy, but I have a home where you can stay as long as you like. My ma would be happy to get you cleaned up and fed. You can stay in one of our spare bedrooms for as long as you like."

"You just can't take this girl to your house, AJ," Luke said after pushing through the small crowd.

"Chief, you've known my family and me my whole life. You know we can take care of her. Ma has taken in more than a few wayward teens over the years. She has a way with people, you know. Also, before my dad died last year, they bought a place in Laguna Palms—a big place with five bedrooms. Ma would probably welcome the company."

"Hmm." Luke wavered. "You mean the new community on the water by the House of Refuge? The old Indian village? I'm surprised the city awarded a permit to build. Last I heard the Indians were fighting for the rights to the land."

"Yeah, that's the place. My pop was one of the first to build a home out there. When it comes to anything in this small town, it's all about the money and who you know."

"Yeah, you got that right," Luke said with a smirk.

"How about this, Chief?" AJ paused and took a deep breath, looking at Luke with genuine concern. "Let me take her home to Ma, then you can come check on her tomorrow. Alright?"

"Alright," Luke agreed. "Tell Ma I'll come if she makes me some of her eucalyptus tea."

"Will do," AJ promised.

AJ kneeled, minimizing his six-foot, rather large frame to make himself less intimidating to the small, frightened girl. In a hushed, calming tone, he asked, "Would it be alright if I drive you to my house? I don't want to seem like I'm whisking you away to a scary place. I need to know that this is alright with you. But please don't be afraid to say no. This has to be your decision. The chief can vouch for me."

The girl's eyes darted back and forth between AJ and Luke. She took a few moments to think about it, then answered with a sulky nod.

"I'll call your ma and tell her you're on your way," the chief offered.

AJ nodded. "Alright then."

On the way home in the car, the girl was silent. AJ didn't press. He was sure she was feeling a little overwhelmed.

When they arrived home, she studied the house with big eyes. The Hudsons' modern two-story home sat upon an acre of land on a hill with dunes and the beach for the backyard. Although she looked frightened, AJ noticed her shoulders settle, and she seemed a bit less timid as they made their way up the stairs and into the house.

Ma greeted the girl at the door with a hug that could smother a bear. "Hello, my lovely, and welcome. The chief just phoned to tell me you will stay with us for a while. Aren't we the lucky ones?"

While Ma was preparing her homemade honey eucalyptus tea in the kitchen, AJ tried to settle the girl's nerves with a joke. "What do you call a pretty girl found at a bus stop?"

She didn't answer, but after a moment, looking down at her hands folded on her lap, said, "What then?"

"A welcomed guest," he answered, and she smiled.

"That's not a joke." She raised her eyes to meet his.

"I suppose not, but it made you smile. I wasn't blessed with my family's good looks or charm, so I thought I could take a shot at humor."

"Well, you're not that funny either." This made AJ laugh out loud.

Since the proverbial ice had been broken, AJ felt comfortable enough to pry a little. "How about you tell me your name?"

"Esther," she said, barely audible.

"Esther, well, it's great to make your acquaintance officially," he said formally, back straight, head held high, and offered his hand. This time, she took his hand and shook it gingerly.

"My ma is great with teenagers like yourself. You'll be happy here while you figure things out," he said sincerely.

"Figure things out?" she asked with a puzzled look.

"Yeah, I'm sure you have plans to get a job, a place of your own someday."

"I suppose." She shrugged her shoulders. "I haven't thought about what comes next. I just knew I had to leave home and my family or I'd have to marry a man I didn't love, that already had several other wives."

"What? Why would your parents force you to marry? Several wives? That's not fair. No wonder you left. You're welcome here, where no one is keen to marry you off." He tried to come across as understanding and compassionate. He recognized from her demeanor that sometimes tragic events cut so profoundly that they scar deeply.

"How old are you? If you don't mind me asking."

"I'm seventeen. Seventeen and a half, actually."

"You look much younger."

"I know. I think that's why I was able to live with my parents for so long."

"What do you mean?"

"Most girls marry at fourteen or fifteen in my community, but thankfully, because I'm small, my parents kept me with them longer until I matured."

"Matured? Um, oh," AJ muttered. Until she got her period, he presumed, but did not say.

"How old are you?" she asked.

"Thirty," he answered.

"Oh, thank you, by the way," she whispered.

"For what?"

"For saving me."

"My pleasure."

"I don't think you're an ordinary guy. You're special. I want you to know that."

"Well, I think you're special too."

"But you're not funny," she said, this time with a larger smile that warmed his heart.

After tea, Ma prepared the spare room, along with the necessary toiletries she kept for emergencies such as this.

Esther showered, put on a pair of Ma's pajamas, and slept soundly for twelve hours.

At eight the following morning, the police chief arrived to check in on Esther. He chatted with Ma in the kitchen for a few minutes. They spoke in hushed tones, and AJ couldn't make out a single word. Initially, he peered in unnoticed. Ma whispered while the chief listened intently, drumming his fingers on the table. Ma sipped her tea as AJ walked into the kitchen toward the coffee pot. Before heading out to work downtown at the courthouse, this was his daily routine. They hushed up as he entered, eyes on AJ as he walked across the kitchen.

"What secret plans are you two conjuring?" he asked playfully. Neither of their faces appeared jovial.

"Okay, then I'll be on my way," he said after he grabbed his briefcase from the kitchen counter.

"The girl, how's she doing?" the chief asked.

"Her name is Esther. She seems alright, considering," AJ offered. "I think she needs some time to decompress from her journey."

"I trust your ma will take great care of her," the chief said, touching Ma's hand with a soft squeeze. It was a little too familiar a gesture for AJ's taste, and now he wondered if Luke had been one of his mom's foster kids or troubled teens she took in for short periods while he was away at school. The chief nodded in Ma's direction as he stood and headed toward the door. "Good luck at your new job as a public defender. I hope you lose every case," he mused, trying to be funny. But in all actuality, he was not joking at all.

"Your prosecutors best be on their toes, Chief, especially if my clients are minors. I'm a formidable opponent. You've been warned."

Chapter Thirteen

Lunch at Pietro's on the River
February 6, 2019
Holly

L adies luncheon is a favorite activity with the girls in the cul-de-sac. The ladies get together the first Wednesday afternoon of every month at 3:30 p.m. It's a late start for most, but they've got to wait for Greta to nap and Chloe to get home from work. Each month, they get together at a different restaurant on the island. Today's reservation is confirmed at Pietro's, and I'm excited as this is my first outing with everyone since I moved in.

"Reservation for four," says Gina.

"Yes, Gina, we have a window table reserved for you ladies. Right this way." The tiny, ninety-five-pound hostess turns and wiggles her way over to our table. At the same time, we follow in single file through the restaurant, trying to imitate her sassy little walk, giggling in unison as most diners finish their desserts and cappuccino.

Gina loves a 3:30 reservation. The lunch crowd settles their checks, and we are left in peace with a nearly empty restaurant, listening to the warm rise and fall of distant conversation and lots of attention from the wait staff.

Immediately after settling into our comfortable chairs, Chloe hands out tiny boxes to each of us. Inside each one is a rock painted by one of her students. Mine is blue with googly eyes. I am sure it's intended to be Cookie Monster. Very cute. Greta's is painted red with googly eyes and black spots, intended to be a ladybug, and Gina's has a daisy painted on it.

"Adorable," Greta says.

"Fabulous. Those kids are talented," says Gina.

"I love it. You are so good with these kids," I say.

"Thank you." Chloe blushes. "I'm proud of them. Keeping my little friends focused on one task is quite a challenge. I've learned never to underestimate the big importance of small things. This piece of art is a great accomplishment for my students. Believe me, I spend a good portion of the day wrangling them to sit still in their seats, and don't get me started about all the ways I try to convince them to keep their shoes on."

"Chloe, you're such a great caregiver. You should have popped out more," I say.

"No way. I'm happy with just Luna. Having come from a family of eleven, one is pure joy!"

"Eleven!" all three of us shout out.

"Yup."

The waiter hears the yelping and quickly walks over, looking past the rest of us like furniture and honing in only on Gina.

"Hello, beautiful. You look lovely this afternoon," says our waiter, Homer, his eyes sparkling like Gina was a celebrity he was dying to meet.

"Hello, Homer." Gina shakes her feathered blonde hair like she just waltzed out of a shampoo commercial and smiles. "So happy you will be our waiter today. Please bring us a bottle of prosecco, would you?"

"My pleasure," he says with a wink.

"Well, *someone* has a crush," Chloe says quietly for only us to hear. I can't help but wonder why anyone would name their child Homer. Such a terrible name. Maybe his parents were fans of *The Simpsons*. Or the literary genius and Greek poet of *The Iliad* and *The Odyssey*. I prefer to believe the latter. I choose this answer to calm my thoughts and stop any further distractions in my mind about his name. My therapist taught me that when I find myself drifting off in thought and contemplating unimportant things, I must force myself to find a solution to my burning questions, however unlikely, and move on to the best of my ability.

Pietro himself delivers the prosecco to the table. He's an adorable little Italian man.

"Hello, Gina," he says, and you can tell he is also smitten with her beauty. "Thank you for bringing the ladies here for lunch today. It's great seeing you again. If you need anything, please let me know, but I am sure Homer will take good care of you." He pours the prosecco for us, then heads back to the kitchen.

It's impressive the way Gina takes command of a room. Even from a restaurant table, her presence makes everyone else seem like wallpaper.

"Wow, you know the owner?" says Chloe.

"Is he a fan of your work?" asks Greta with a sly smirk.

"Oh, no. He's such a sweet old man. I just come here often," Gina says with a wink. Then she changes the subject and suggests, "You have all got to try my favorite salad, the island chicken salad. It comes with gorgonzola cheese, granny smith apples, and candied walnuts, served with key lime vinaigrette."

"Yes, order for us all," Greta says. "Extra walnuts. And thank you, Chloe, for the gifts. I have a gift as well. A stock tip for you ladies if you are interested."

"Do tell," I say.

"Vertex Pharmaceuticals is about to skyrocket. You didn't hear this from me, so it's definitely *not* insider trading…but they have a few new drugs that just hit the market that will help people with cystic fibrosis live decades longer by correcting the underlying genetic defect."

Crickets. No one says a word.

"Okay, ladies. Just a tip for you to make a bit of money. Can you at least pretend to be interested in making money instead of spending it?"

"Thank you, Greta," says Chloe with as big a smile as she can muster. "Yes, of course, we can pretend to care about the stock market."

"Alright, I'll buy a thousand shares tomorrow," says Gina, rolling her eyes. "Right after, I take my flying pig out for a spin. I'm kidding. You know this and thank you. I'll tell my financial advisor."

Not enjoying Gina's humor, Greta speaks now in her bossy, corporate voice. "I was just trying to look out for you all. It's a good tip. This hundred-and-ninety-dollar stock will most likely double in the next five years. You WILL make money. Chloe gave us kindergarten trinkets. I give you stock tips, but as usual, Chloe's gifts are always best."

Gina responds, "Of course they are. They're made with love from our youngest humans. Someone's a bit testy today."

When the salads arrive, the apples and the extra candied walnuts remind me of the fruitcake that killed Patty.

Chloe must have been thinking along those same lines because she suggests, "Let's make a toast to Patty. This is our first ladies' outing without her." We raise our glasses in unison, clink, and sip.

"As a tribute, we should continue the fruitcake exchange this year," Gina proposes.

"Oh, hell no," Greta barks back with a sharp shake of her head, hair tossing out of place from its perfect blunt cut, long strands of hair tumbling over her short bangs. She's angry. "This is not a good idea. It could lead to further catastrophe." Irritation dances in her voice.

"We have to. It was her idea. And let's continue her vision," Gina says flatly, in a matter-of-fact way, as if all further discussion is pointless.

"What vision?" Greta asks, fiddling with her bracelet and fidgeting in her chair.

"She had this vision that everyone in the community would look out for one another," Gina explains.

"I'm sorry, please excuse me." Greta stands. "I have to go to the ladies' room."

"What's wrong with her?" asks Chloe as Greta flees, stomping away.

"No idea," I say, but I'm worried she is still a bit freaked out about Patty's death. From what I understand, Patty spent a lot of time at the Barneses' house when Harrington needed a babysitter.

"Greta is always a bit irritated about something or other. Don't take it personally, ladies," Gina says, brushing off Greta's theatrics.

Upon Greta's return, Chloe offers, "Let's make a pact not to waste today in sadness about yesterday. Alright, ladies?"

"Yes," we all agree.

"Well said," Gina says, reapplying her ruby-red lipstick and looking for Homer for a bottle refresh.

Deep into our second bottle of prosecco, Chloe asks me, "So, how did you and Bradley meet?"

"Holly is a singer-songwriter," says Gina.

"Really?"

"Really," I say. "I was auditioning for a Sony record deal when Bradley walked in to speak with the music producer about another artist. He sat for my audition and asked me out for a drink when I finished."

"That's so romantic." Chloe swoons, hugging herself with both arms. "Did you get the contract?"

"No. Sadly, the world is harsh to artists who are good but not truly great. I did, however, catch a very hot husband."

"Yes, indeed," says Gina. "And don't be so hard on yourself. I'm sure that your talent is worthy of a professional contract."

"I'm not sure about that. There are so many brilliant artists being discovered every day on social media. Enough about that. Bradley said something to me in the studio that I'll never forget."

"Spill it," says Gina.

"When he asked me out for a drink, initially I turned him down, told him that I was recovering from a broken heart, but hold on for his response. He said, 'I never trust anyone who hasn't had their heart broken in all the right places.' Right there, I knew I wanted to marry this guy."

"Goosebumps." Chloe shows us the tiny little bumps on her arm.

"Of course, as a music producer," I explain, "he revels in the pain of artists to elicit something meaningful . . . magic. But it was the way he delivered that line. He looked right into my eyes like no one else was in the room."

"So much can be learned from endings and new beginnings," Gina says with such wisdom it lands heavily on our shoulders, and we ponder silently for a few moments.

"Do you think you will ever return to that industry?" asks Chloe, hoping for an answer I cannot deliver.

"No. After having three kids and the fact that I'll be thirty next year, it's probably too late for me," I admit reluctantly while searching through my phone for a photo of my demo album cover, titled Adrift with Holly Helena. I show the image to the ladies, then explain, "I recorded the album at Mr. 305 studios, on Twelfth Street in Miami. You know, Pitbull's recording studio. By the way, there is no better talent or kinder person from Miami. Their parent company is Sony."

Gina grabs the phone from my hand for a closer look.

"Anywho, the album is pop with a Cuban vibe, a throwback to my dad's side of the family."

"Girl, I had no idea you were Cuban. The things you learn about a lady over a few cocktails," says Gina, throwing up her right hand and letting it fall limp.

"My grandfather's version of the story is grim, providing fodder for childhood nightmares, but the short version is that he drifted here on a raft from Cuba many years ago. My grandfather made it to shore while his two brothers and sister perished from dehydration, delirium, and tiger sharks. It may only be ninety miles from Florida, but the conditions are treacherous."

"What? Oh my! I can't even imagine surviving such a traumatic journey. Devastating," says Chloe.

"Such a terrible tragedy," says Greta. "So sorry for your family."

Gina, hardly paying attention to my story, blurts out, "Wow, you look so different with platinum blonde hair," referring to the album cover. "You should dye it blonde again. The color is stunning on you."

"Definitely," Greta agrees.

"Maybe one day," I say.

"You are beautiful no matter the color of your hair." You can always count on Chloe for a compliment when you're most in need of one. She grins. I return a smile.

Now I have to change the subject—too much attention on me. I hate that. I ask Gina, "Have you ever been married?" Strange way to steer a conversation, I'm aware, but I had to change the focus of the discussion. I panicked—stupid question.

"Married? Me?" she says, feigning shock. "Well, yes. Interesting story. I was married once when I was nineteen, to one of the VPs of MGM Studios, forty years my senior. He put my name on the map as a runway model. I was doing print ads at the time. I wanted it all," she says proudly. "Don't judge me. Not everyone can make it on their own. Some of us have to hitch a ride along the way. What did Marie Antoinette once say? Oh yeah: You can have your cake and take his money too!" I reckon we all laugh a bit too loudly because the ladies across from us snicker.

I whirl my head around and notice that they are quietly talking about us. I ask in a whisper, "Who are they?"

"Those eight ladies are The Nanas from Nettles Island. They host their book club here every month. They must be very busy talking about some dumb romance novel," Gina suggests.

"Romance novel? Hardly. I am going to go with something really smutty, like *Fifty Shades of Grey*," offers Chloe.

"Smut is what the kindergarten teacher suggests? Funny!" I say with a smirk. "My guess is those ladies are a bit progressive. Look at how cute they are. Most of them are wearing pink and yellow Lily Pulitzer dresses. They're drinking mojitos and flirting with Homer. I'll say *The Handmaid's Tale*. What do you think, Greta?"

Greta sighs. Her eyes scan their faces and the book in the center of their table. Then she says,

"I'm going with *The Nightingale.* Looks like a big book, and that one is really popular right now."

"Interesting," says Gina.

Gina returns to the previous conversation by hinting in my direction. "You know, if you want something bad enough, the universe arranges it."

"Thank you, Gina. I appreciate that." Suddenly, I am a bit overwhelmed with emotion that I didn't know I was holding back. A wave of nostalgia creeps over me, and I release a single tear. I feel all eyes on me now.

"Sorry for falling apart," I say, wiping away the stray tear, careful not to smear my mascara. "I should hold myself together better. I miss music and singing. Well, I miss those days a lot. These days are all mess and mayhem with my little maniacs."

"It's okay. Tacos fall apart sometimes, too, and we still love them." Chloe smiles. A vision of the gnome in her front yard holding tacos makes me happy while her smile melts my heart, and suddenly I feel better.

Chloe, always the one to steer every conversation into a happier place, says, "Have I ever told you ladies how I almost got fired for roofies?

"What?" "No way" and "Shut up" are the responses from the rest of us.

Chloe shrugs, twists her long ponytail with her fingers, and begins.

"Well, one-day last year, after recess, I poured lemonade for my kiddos at the picnic table before heading back into the classroom. One of the girls, Hayley, tells me, 'Ms. Chloe, I'm not drinking that. How do I know you didn't put roofies in there?' Now, I'm shocked. Flabbergasted, really. Of course, the rest of the kids chime in. 'Ms. Chloe, what are roofies?' To which I answer, 'You'll have to ask your mom,' while shuffling the kids back into class.

"Needless to say, my phone and email blew up that evening. The conversation with my principal the following morning was not pleasant."

Chloe looks at me and smiles. I nod, my way of thanking her for steering the conversation elsewhere while I pull myself together. She really is the sweetest!

"What was I supposed to say? Should I have lied and said a roofie was someone who fixes a leak in your roof? Ugh, kids sure do say the darnedest things," she sings in a slightly high-pitched voice.

"Tell me more about your first husband, Gina," Chloe asks, allowing me even more time to get myself together.

"Well, at first, he was really into me, but after a few years, he seemed disinterested. So I bought some shackles and a flogger, which changed everything."

"What, now?"

"Huh?"

"Oh my!"

We all interject in a similar fashion.

"I've learned two things about men," Gina begins. "Firstly, men are like handbags. They serve a purpose but can easily be replaced the following season. Secondly, most men want to be dominated. It's a mommy thing," Gina continues. "You, of all people, should know how men are, Greta. You work in the financial industry. Totally male-dominated."

"Yes, but—"

Homer walks over and asks, "Hey, ladies, I meant to ask you what happened to the guy that went missing in your neighborhood over the weekend?"

"We don't know much." Gina exhales loudly. "A police officer took our statements, but we haven't heard anything yet. How did you hear about that?"

"I go to school with Chet. He's staying with his uncle right now. We're all hoping for the best."

"I'm sure he will turn up soon," says Chloe.

I glance at the time on my phone. "We gotta go. The savages will be home soon."

"Okay, but before we leave," Gina begs, "we've got to hear more about your siblings, Chloe."

"Not much to tell. My mom wanted a big family, and my dad wanted lots of doctors, lawyers, and teachers to continue our family's pristine reputation in these parts. That's enough about me." Chloe turns her attention to me. "Holly, sing us a little ditty. Please?"

Feeling a bit tipsy, I oblige. "My favorite is to sing impromptu, Eminem style. You know, like in the movie *8 Mile*." I think briefly, then tell the ladies, "Pick a subject."

"Um, friendship," Greta offers.

"Alright then," I say. Suddenly, drenched with creativity, wine-drunk, I feel alive. "Imagine I'm playing this on my guitar:

Gina, Chloe, and Greta, three friends I adore,
Living in Laguna Palms on Hutchinson Island shore.
Our bond of friendship will never fade,
As we hold each other close, forever more.
Friends are the family we choose,
No matter what life throws at you.
We will always be there,
For each other forever more, forever more.

Our friendship is a treasure,
Priceless and true.
Forever grateful,
For every one of you.

Friends are the family we choose,
No matter what life throws at you.
We will always be there,
For each other forever more, forever more."

I stand up, curtsey, placing my right foot behind my left, and nearly fall over—a bit too much prosecco. I reach out for my chair for support. Soft clapping can be heard from a few patrons at nearby tables. I turn and smile.

"That was cringey. That song is cheesy, like a cheap hallmark card. Simply terrible. I loved it!" squeals Gina.

Gina casually motions for the check with her right index finger and pays with her American Express Black Card. We gather our cell phones and purses from the table.

While walking out of Pietro's, I stop at the Nanas' table to apologize for the noise and distraction. Chloe elbows me in the ribs, and I notice that the book of the month is *Fifty Shades*

Freed, the third book in the trilogy. Oh shit, she was right . . . smut, indeed.

On the Uber ride home, Gina tells the driver to stop at Strawberry's, the ice cream parlor on the island. Gina hardly ate, but now she wants ice cream?

"You have terrible eating habits." I stammer and slur the words while resting my head on Chloe's shoulder. Greta and Chloe nod in agreement.

"Yeah, it's a supermodel thing."

Chapter Fourteen

Harry Returns
February 7, 2019
Holly

The average person will encounter four to six different turning points within their lifetime. College, career changes, marriage, divorce, and retirement are common turning points people experience. Other, less common turning point examples could be the challenging climb out of drug use or alcohol addiction, sexual abuse, et cetera. Turning points are initiated by a crisis or a time of deep reflection when we feel our lives unraveling. New decisions are made to help get your life back on track and steer yourself in a new direction.

Four days after Harry disappeared, he returned home without mentioning what happened, why he left, or what occurred while he was gone. He returned as nonchalantly as he disappeared, like a poof of smoke from a magician. Chet went door-to-door in the cul-de-sac to inform everyone that he returned home safely.

While I witness Harry drive in and out of his garage daily, he hasn't spoken to anyone since he came home, not even Chloe's husband, Fred.

Collectively, we decide not to pry and allow him time to process whatever has transpired. Since he is closest to Fred, I expect to hear any information about Harry from Chloe as soon as she has anything interesting to report.

Six months pass, and still, no one talks about what happened to Harry during those four days. There have been attempts by Fred and Bradley to get him out of the house. He never answers the door. Chet told Luna that his dad is doing well, but he is not quite the same. He seems sullen, sad, and even quit his job for a new one.

However, there has been gossip in the neighborhood—lots of strange abduction stories. Willa, who lives a few doors down from me and whom I met one day at the park while my kids were petting her doggies, suggests that maybe Harry was taken by the same people who kidnapped a teenager from the neighborhood.

"Sam, a seventeen-year-old drug addict, disappeared for two weeks over Christmas break in 2015," she tells me. "His parents were frantic. Police said he probably ran away or overdosed on drugs, but here is where the story gets weird. Two weeks later, he comes home. He rings the doorbell freshly shaven, hair cut, clean clothes, and says he never felt better. Soon after, he took the ACT, got a thirty-two, applied to college, and off he went over the summer to Florida State. He's in law school now at the University of Florida."

"So what happened to him in those two weeks to straighten him out? Could his parents have sent him off somewhere to get help?" I ask Willa.

"Hardly. If so, they would not have involved the police and the whole community trying to find him. They even pleaded with the locals for help on the evening news," she explains.

"So what do *you* think happened to him?"

"No one knows, but this instance is eerily similar to Harry's disappearance. One day, they disappear and come back seemingly different people. Very strange."

"Very strange, indeed."

Chapter Fifteen

The Decision
December 6, 2022
The Captive

I'm not one to beat about the bush. It's already been six days since I've seen the light of day. I decide to fess up to four terrible transgressions, a few of which I have never uttered aloud to anyone. I could admit to one or two, but my gut tells me it's best to be honest in my apparent situation to survive. I had almost forgotten about the few assisted suicides. I'll have to fess up to those as well. I remember the hologram said explicitly that a few people have perished, so I must be forthcoming.

I'm flooded with sadness and confusion within these long days and nights of solitude. The quiet forces you to realize how much noise there is in the world. I lay in bed for what seems like an eternity before I can focus on my feelings. Peacefulness surrounds me suddenly, softening the weight of my sorrow. But this stillness brings back painful memories I have been trying to push back into the dark recesses of my mind. Instead of hiding from the pain, the silence forces me to face the hurt all over again. A long-buried memory rises to the surface. The memories you can recall when the world grows silent are genuinely amazing. I stare at the scar on my left hand. The scar my sister left me. It's disturbing watching your own body offer clues to forgotten childhood trauma. Memories begin to flood my brain. I recall my sister gathering coloring books and puzzles, pushing me into our parents' closet whenever she brought friends over. I remember pleading with her.

"I won't tell, I won't tell, please let me out!" To throw extra fuel on the fire, she would leave me with a portable TV and VHS tapes of horror movies to keep me company. I can now come to terms with my love-hate relationship with scary movies. Those movies comforted me in those moments, however, I was terrified by the content. I watched *The Exorcist* and *The Shining* more times than I can recollect.

As I stare at my scar, I recall the last time she trapped me in the closet. I took hold of a coat hanger and jammed it into the lock until it finally opened for me. I raced down the stairs, only to find my terrible sister and her friends smoking weed and drinking beer on the terrace. She threw an empty beer bottle at me when she spotted me in the kitchen. I raised my hand to catch it. It shattered instead on the floor by my feet. I should have run off, but instinctively, I dropped to the floor to clean it up, thinking only that Mom would be mad if she found a mess. I grabbed a large glass shard. Blood trickled, then flowed. The smell of copper and the dizziness is all I remember. I woke up in the ER, needing twelve stitches. The bully eventually forgets their awful behavior, but the victim never does. I still hate her.

Enough about childhood memories. I push them back. I dig deep into my Catholic values, which weigh heavily on my soul. I lie here and contemplate all of my indiscretions. Some are harder to come to terms with than others.

As a kid, you're afraid of the menacing monster in the closet and shadows in the darkness. But what happens if that monster turns out to be you? This is a truth that's hard to grasp. How exactly did my life go to shit?

Here in the dead of night, there is just one thing that I can hold on to. It's a sentiment or truth of my faith. *God always shows up on time*. At least, that's what I've been told. Help is on the way. I must have hope, at least a glimpse of it. Hope is the only thing I can hold on to. Even the word gives me solace. *Hope*.

Will it be today? Tomorrow? Sometime next week? I'm unsure, but I feel comforted knowing I'll be saved someday.

"Alright," I yell out, "I am ready to tell you all the terrible things I've done. Hello? Are you there?"

Chapter Sixteen

The Wedding
November 1983
Judge Hudson

L ife is full of contradictions. AJ was often brought back to an idea he discussed at length in law school regarding chaos theory, or more specifically, order versus chaos in the law. How can one beautiful, typical, small thing lead to something sinister? Most people are familiar with the butterfly effect, a scenario in which a butterfly flaps its wings in Africa, and that small change in the atmosphere leads to other minor changes that could unleash a tornado in Texas. The idea could also work in the opposite direction. How can one sinister act lead to something extraordinary? For one example, a deadly car accident in which passengers were ejected and killed led to the invention of the seatbelt. Another, the brutal beatings of the 1965 "Bloody Sunday" civil rights march from Selma to Montgomery, led to the passage of the Voting Rights Act three months later.

AJ had only ever craved stability and structure. He only ever wanted a simple life on the beach, fighting for justice for those who couldn't afford their own counsel. But life threw unexpected events and uncertainty as a catalyst, forcing growth and change. In the end, it's the chaos that leads to the order we seek. That was his theory, anyway. His life was no different than the contradictory universal order of things.

While AJ worked twelve-hour days in the public defender's office, Ma mentored Esther.

"So, what are your goals? How can I help you achieve them?" Ma made it her mission to care for this girl.

"Well, I would like to finish high school and learn more about gardening and cooking."

Ma helped Esther obtain her GED. In her spare time, Esther assisted with the cooking, household chores and in the garden, tending to tomatoes, cucumbers, peppers, and lettuce. Ma's favorite plants were purple periwinkles, which flourished throughout the backyard. Esther tended to Ma's plants like they were her children. She also agreed to paint the beachside wooden picket fence, a lovely seafoam green to match the color of the ocean, which delighted Ma.

Several months passed, and they celebrated Esther's eighteenth birthday with a three-layer cake Ma made from scratch. But they heard a loud thud at the door before Esther could blow out the candles—an aggressive knock, followed by three more frantic thumps.

Ma shrieked, "What in all tarnation is going on? AJ, go answer the door! Someone must be bloodied or half dead out there."

AJ opened the door to a small woman in a prairie dress, French braid, no makeup, and a larger man in a blue suit, no tie.

"May I help you?" AJ asked politely.

"We're here for Esther," the man claimed. But AJ already knew that by the looks of them. The way they were dressed, they could only be here to collect their daughter for some sick cult offering.

"She's not he—"

AJ was cut off by Esther, who had snuck up on him from behind.

"I'm not leaving," she said defiantly, hands on her hips. Angry, she added, "How did you know I was here?"

"You called your little sister. She told us," her mom explained.

"I didn't want her to worry, is all."

"We're all worried. Now pack up, and let's go home," her mom demanded. "You had your fun. Now it's time to go home."

"No," Esther insisted. "I can't."

"Well, why—pray tell—not?" Her mom was getting miffed at her resistance. Her cheeks turned a bright red. "You must return home or be excommunicated from the community."

"I'm married," Esther blurted out.

"Married?" Her mom looked like she might faint and grabbed her husband's arm for support.

"Yes. Married."

AJ's face turned as red as Esther's mom's. But he manned up, straightened his shoulders, and defended Esther.

"Yes, we're married," he lied and instantly felt a sense of pride in lying about this. He felt as though his lie was noble. He thought, who do they think they are, collecting her to marry her off to some creep?

"If that's true," her dad suggested, "I'd like to see the marriage certificate. I'll need a copy of it to return home."

"Uh . . . um . . . it's not finalized and signed yet." AJ wavered. "But I can pick it up at City Hall in the morning."

"Alright. Until then, we will be staying at the Holiday Inn here on the island," her dad said with disdain. "We'll be back in the morning," he promised.

"Lovely to have you," AJ smirked. "Ma will prepare breakfast for us. See you then." He smiled as they walked off toward their station wagon parked in the driveway.

"Shoot, what now?" Esther asked.

"We get married, of course."

"Really? Are you sure you want to do this?"

"Yes," AJ agreed. "You left Utah months ago so that you wouldn't have to get married. Are you absolutely sure *you* want to do this?"

"I like it here. I love Ma, and I want to do this. I can't go back. I won't go back. But . . . I don't want to corner you or make you do something you don't want to do."

"Well, honestly, I never really thought of you that way. I think of you like a sister I never had, but I will marry you so that you can escape this terrible situation."

AJ paused momentarily to collect his thoughts and then professed, "When I met you at the bus stop, I decided to save you, so I'll happily follow through with that promise. But I must tell you, I've only had a few real girlfriends and not many friends. Most people say I'm dull, boring. I'm not an emotional man. But I'm loyal and reliable. I am very good at what I do, and my love for the law and the community I serve is pure. Also, I work long hours. I'm not home much. You'll have to learn to make do on your own. My only wish is that, over time, we may become great friends. The greatest relationships are sustained by great friendships—oh, and mutual respect, of course.

But I won't push. No pressure. Anyway, if you are, I'm in this all the way."

"Thank you," Esther said sincerely and hugged him so tightly it hurt.

"I'll call my friend I went to high school with. He's the commissioner," he squeaked out while being smushed.

Commissioner Alan Smith arrived a few hours later. In her excitement, Ma demanded Esther wear her wedding dress and pose for more pictures than they were comfortable with.

"I'm so excited for the two of you. Esther, I want you to wear my wedding band for the ceremony, and AJ, you can wear your dad's. He would be so proud of you, AJ. I wish he were here to witness this."

"Thank you, Ma." He inspected both rings and immediately began to feel like today, this moment, was meant to be. These rings were meant for them to inherit.

"Who would have imagined that the first girl AJ brings home, he marries?" said Ma with such enthusiasm she seemed like she would explode.

Ma assembled an exquisite bouquet of roses and orchids from the garden. The moon provided a perfect spotlight and backdrop for an intimate, unexpected evening under the stars on the beach.

"To the beginning of the rest of our lives," Esther whispered in AJ's ear before the commissioner said, "You may kiss the bride."

"I hope to be the man you expect me to be—for you and our family," AJ replied before kissing his new bride. Like nature's confetti, a gust of wind blew yellow petals toward them as they kissed—a gift from Ma's backyard *Tabebuia* tree.

The three sat quietly in the kitchen the following morning, drinking tea. Ma had prepared her famous sausage, egg, and cheese casserole with biscuits and gravy. They waited patiently for Esther's parents. When they didn't show up to collect a copy of the marriage certificate, AJ called the Holiday Inn to learn only that they never checked in. Somehow, he was not surprised.

At first, the marriage was an obligation, but over time, within a year and every day that followed, AJ grew to love Esther more than he thought it was possible to love another person.

AJ often pondered the chaos theory he learned in law school, acknowledging that the chaos of Esther's life brought joy to his own. Because he met Esther, his life moving forward would never be the same. He and Esther bonded over the love of family and an affinity for helping others less fortunate. Every time a broken, abandoned, or battered child found himself or herself in AJ's courtroom, Esther wanted desperately to foster the child, a trait she picked up from Ma. Over the years, Ma had taken in many wayward teens her husband brought home from his own courtroom, so in that respect, the apple doesn't fall far from the tree.

Over the next ten years, they fostered eleven children. Although many didn't stay long, Esther made quite an impression before they were placed with permanent families. The kids and teens kept in touch with both Esther and Ma often. Esther became attached to all of them not only because she had a heart of gold but also as a distraction, as they had not been graced with children of their own. She understood this to mean that this must be God's will. She believed her life's work, putting back the pieces of broken children, could not be carried out if she had children of her own. At one point, they had so many children living with them, eight at one time, that she had AJ build four additional rooms in the basement.

Esther may have been small, but she had quite a heavy hand for such a tiny lady. She demanded respect from the kids, discipline, and a future plan before they were placed in a forever home. She insisted they choose a career path that would make the community a better place. This, she may have harvested from her time in her cult. The community she grew up in promoted discipline and a purposeful work ethic. Old habits die hard.

AJ never questioned how Esther disciplined the foster kids, even when she converted one of the rooms in the basement into a jail of sorts. She labeled it The Rehabilitation Room, where a few found themselves when they disobeyed or disrespected her or Ma's wishes. She was not one to raise a hand to the kids, but solitary confinement quickly turned some of the more challenging teenagers around. AJ never questioned her judgment. It was his job to rescue kids, and her job to raise them.

Chapter Seventeen

A New Puppy for Chet
Halloween 2019
Holly

When Halloween rolls around, and everyone is setting their tables and chairs around the cul-de-sac for this evening's trick-or-treat festivities, along comes Chet with what looks like a three-month-old golden retriever.

"I love your new puppy," I say.

"She's a bit termagant."

I smile because he must have really had to graze through his SAT file in his mind to come up with that one. So I play along.

"Yes, new puppies can often be a bit recalcitrant when they are little. They are quite rambunctious. Lots of energy to expel, and they have difficulty containing their energy or impulse control. A few months and a bit of discipline, she'll be your best friend in no time."

He smiles back. I'm sure he has no idea what recalcitrant means. I'm hoping he'll google it later.

"My dad bought her for me," he says excitedly.

I lean in and pet her. She wiggles her tail. Chet should be happier than he looks. I tilt my head, trying to read his face.

Luna approaches us. "Hey, Chet, nice pup. What's her name?"

"Goldy."

"How's your dad?" she asks, kneeling on the sidewalk to pet the puppy.

"Hasn't said much since he came home. He seems fine, but some things are strange."

"Strange? How do you mean?" I ask.

"Well, he quit his job. Now he works for a nonprofit acquisition company that acquires space for Boys & Girls Clubs, charities, or law firms that work mostly pro bono."

"That sounds great," I say. "That's much better work than buying companies and selling them off in parts to the highest bidder."

"Oh, sure. No doubt. Totally. He's much nicer now but rarely jokes around anymore, so I worry about him. He hasn't been out of the house at all to play golf with the guys or . . . well, or anything."

"Why not?" I ask. I made a mental note to ask Chloe to tell Fred to reach out to him more forcefully soon.

"I think he's ashamed or doesn't want people to know what happened to him or something like that."

"Did he tell you anything about those four days?" I clench my teeth three times, another way to squelch my anxiety when hearing disturbing news or feeling uneasy or unsettled.

"No, but after he came home, I noticed he was missing his pinky finger."

"Wha—" But I am interrupted.

"Holly—um, Ms. Kelly?" Chet points across the street. "Isn't that one of your kids standing in the bay window naked? What is he wiping on the glass? Is that poo?"

I swivel my head toward home. Yup, that's Rosco, fully naked, wearing only his Iron Man mask. That kid is not quite right. Just yesterday, he wanted to know why his penis can't come out and see people.

"I'm sorry," I say. "Gotta go and take care of this! Talk soon."

Chapter Eighteen

Trick or Treat
Halloween 2019
Holly

Halloween. A special time of year when children transform themselves by donning costumes that emulate their favorite characters or spookiest creature getup and venture off into the neighborhood, creating lasting childhood memories that they will cherish for the rest of their lives.

By 6:00 p.m., all of the kids in the cul-de-sac are ready to roll through the neighborhood in search of sugary treats, and who can resist the excitement of Hershey's candy bars, gummy worms, Skittles, and candy corn?

Chloe took Luna to a sleepover, so it will just be the Barnes and Kelly families this evening.

Rosco is dressed as Iron Man, Emmett is Spider-Man, and Rosie is dressed as a bunny because, you know, superheroes are stupid. "They destroy the entire city just to kill one bad guy," she says.

Ana and Eva are dressed as two little bears, Greta is Goldilocks, and Harrington is the Big Bad

Wolf. The costumes were handmade by Harrington. So, apparently, he can sew too. There may be nothing this man cannot do. Very impressive.

Since the kids are still a bit young to walk so many blocks, Harrington packs all the kiddos into one of Fred's brilliantly designed golf carts with an additional third row. With the press of a button, Harrington transforms the cart into a Halloween party bus. All the children jump about excitedly, clapping their hands, dancing around, and spinning in circles with delight, making little Eva fall over with dizziness. Rosco bangs his head on the sidewalk while trying to complete a somersault and misjudging the distance to the curb.

"Can't we make it through one little evening without an injury, kids? Let's be on our best behavior tonight. Please?" I beg.

At the first stop, Harrington, Greta, and I are handed bottles of Angry Orchid hard cider, and the kids have to knock on a coffin in the middle of the yard, out of which a vampire pops to offer them a handful of candy. The kids get such a kick out of that— they get to do it twice.

The next house delights us adults with orange Jell-O shots, and the kids get to walk through a haunted garage with ghosts flying about like the dementors in *Harry Potter*.

An hour into the evening, and about twenty houses later, we stop at Dr. Davis's house. It's a spectacular home with a gorgeous fountain and waterfall at the entrance.

"Here we are," says Greta. "The home of Dr. Delicious. At least, that's what the ladies in the neighborhood call him. He's movie star-level handsome and quite the catch. I hear he gets around with the ladies if you know what I mean."

"Dr. Delicious? Seriously? Is this season seventeen of *Grey's Anatomy*?"

My phone rings suddenly. It's Bradley.

"Hey, you," I answer.

"Happy Halloween, love. Sorry I couldn't be there," he says, and I can hear the sadness in his voice.

"When we return, I'll have the kids call you and tell you about the evening. They're having a blast."

I hear a splash and a thud, and I am not surprised that Rosco has fallen or jumped into the fountain. Eva starts running toward the fountain, and Harrington picks her up just in time. Rosie breaks out in laughter, forever entertained by her brother's antics.

"I've got to go. The kids are on a tear, and Rosco took it upon himself to bathe in Dr. Davis's fountain. I've got my hands full. Talk later. Love you and miss you terribly."

"Same."

"I suppose it's time to head back," says Greta, stating the obvious.

As we return to the cul-de-sac, Greta suggests, "Hey, let's go to the Hudson house. That place is creepy enough for Halloween."

"Sure, let's go," I say, but as soon as we turn around the circle, their porch lights flicker and then turn off, and the sprinklers come on full force as if to say, "Stay the fuck away! Fuck off!"

"Rude!" Greta yells out.

"Stupid, creepy bitches," I say under my breath, intending for only Greta to hear.

Rosie turns her head my way and says, "That's not very nice, Mommy."

When we return to my house to say goodbye, Emmett hugs Ana and kisses her on the cheek.

"Oh my, we have a little love affair brewing here," whispers Greta in my ear.

I shrug and say, "I'm so sorry. I hope we can still be friends."

Chapter Nineteen

The Confession
December 7, 2022
The Captive

I awake at 3:00 a.m. to the sound of a trumpet, then a drum roll. Such theatrics! Someone is enjoying this!

"It's time for you to confess," says a lovely female voice from a speaker I still cannot find.

"Alright."

"I must advise you that, like the FBI, we ask questions we already know the answers to, so be careful not to lie. Lying has consequences you may not appreciate if you enjoy using your phalanges."

At that comment, I laugh a little.

"That was not meant to be humorous," she warns.

"A bit of humor is the only mechanism I have left to withstand this rewarding experience you have created for me."

"Your wit and sarcasm are not helpful. Please begin."

"Where should I start?"

"At the beginning, of course."

"Of course. Well, when I was seven—"

A horribly loud horn filled the room for ten seconds.

"Don't be cute. You know what I mean. Let's start four years back."

"Alright, here goes. I killed my first patient. Or rather, I helped to kill my first patient because he had stage four pancreatic cancer."

Horn.

"Try again."

"I need to gather my thoughts here for a moment," I shout.

"Nope. You had plenty of time to reflect. Continue."

My hands shake without my permission. My heart skips in my chest, but I push past the dread I feel in the pit of my stomach and just say it.

"I killed my first patient in 2018."

It was harder than I thought to say those words out loud. I take a deep breath of stagnant basement air and continue.

"He was brought into the emergency room with a gunshot wound, and I may have waited a bit too long to begin the surgery, and he coded on the table just before we began."

"Thank you. See? That was not so difficult. What you did *not* know about your patient is that his wife shot him in cold blood. His wife may have claimed it was self-defense, but that, Dr. Davis, would be incorrect. You may think you have all the answers but you are not God. You took the Hippocratic oath to help people, and clearly, in this instance, you are an accomplice in his death."

"I know his wife. I can't imagine she would do such a thing!"

Horn again.

"Another lie. I warned you. No more lies."

"Okay, no more lies. We were having an affair. She said he hit her and hurt her verbally and physically. I thought this may not be true, but I was selfish when her husband entered the ER. I wanted to protect her . . . and our relationship and I let him die."

"Thank you for your honesty. That's enough for today. For the record, she's the former police chief's niece. She most likely would have gotten away with shooting him without your interference. We will continue our work here tomorrow. It is only through contemplation and madness that your true soul is revealed. Please spend the day reflecting upon your poor judgment, and we will continue again tomorrow."

Silence fills the room for ten seconds. I can't account for the concept of time any longer. She then offers softly, sincerely, "Embrace this part of your journey, my friend. Good day, and rest easy."

Chapter Twenty

The Italian Fruitcake
Christmas Eve 2019

C hloe volunteers to make the fruitcake this year. She'll deliver it to Harry and Chet. It's been quite some time since anyone has spoken with either of them, so this may be a nice gesture from the community.

While Chloe's background is of English, Irish, Scottish, and Italian descent, 23andMe DNA testing proves that she is Italian primarily by just a few percentage points. She decides to make an Italian fruitcake, a panettone, for the Christmas exchange.

In the Italian tradition, the panettone is the quintessential holiday cake. It's an old-world version of the fruitcake, dating back to the Middle Ages. The legend of the panettone can be traced back to an epic love story between a nobleman and the beautiful daughter of a local baker.

According to legend, Ughetto falls in love with the baker's daughter. When the bakery falls upon hard times, Ughetto provides rescue with a more flavorful recipe of his personal version of the panettone by adding a few essential ingredients like raisins, sugar, and candied orange peel. The cake is a hit, and shortly after, Ughetto receives the family's blessing for marriage.

For Italians, panettone cake is all about memories; one bite is all it takes to bring back happy childhood memories. Having grown up in a large family, the panettone brings back a warm memory for Chloe. The cake is centered on the dessert table on Christmas Eve amongst eclairs and multiple Italian cookies and pastries. Her aunts and uncles would chat for hours before her dad pushed everyone toward the door at 11:00 p.m. because Santa was on his way. So says NORAD's Santa tracker.

Chloe finds a recipe for a panettone fruitcake made with toasted hazelnuts and chocolate on *Food & Wine* magazine's website. The recipe is quite complicated, which is a challenge Chloe enjoys.

After two full days of preparing and baking the panettone, the cake sits beautifully upon a crystal cake dish gifted to her at her bridal shower from a great-aunt she never met.

"Hey, Mom, I'm home," Luna calls out, returning from her tennis lesson this morning with a handful of candy canes.

"Hey, baby, the cake is ready. Come look."

"It's beautiful, Mom. You really do have a talent for baking. This morning, one of the ladies at the court gave me some candy canes. Did you know that two million candy canes are made every year? Benedictine monks invented them in the early seventeenth century. Then, in 1670, a choirmaster in Germany decided to bend the peppermint stick like a shepherd's hook to better fit into the Christmas nativity theme. The stripes were added later."

"Fascinating, Luna. Would you like to come with me to deliver the cake to Harry and Chet? And how was your tennis lesson?"

"Yeah, I'll go. The lesson was fine, but have you ever really listened to neighbors' conversations? They are so remedial. Both the ladies and the men talk about really uninteresting things. I'm not sure I want to grow old."

"What do you mean?"

"Well, the conversations I overheard today during my lesson went something like this:

'Great weather we're having.'

'When is the garbage pickup this week? Is it different because of the holiday?'

'Did you notice how much the real estate taxes increased this year?'

"So boring. Teenagers are much more articulate and profound. We care about things like social issues, the environment, and the planet's future health. It's just an observation."

Laughing, Chloe agrees. "We adults can never compete with kids' intelligence, creativity, and social awareness today, for sure. Let's walk over to Harry's. You ready?"

"Sure."

They ring the doorbell and Chet answers. "Hey, Luna . . . Mrs. Brown."

"Hey, Chet."

"Your turn for the fruitcake this year, I see."

"Yup, it's got to be delicious since my Mom made it."

"No doubt. Thank you," he says to both Chloe and Luna. "We could really use the good luck this year."

Goldy rushes to the door and jumps on Luna.

"Hey, Goldy," Luna says, petting her head.

"No, Goldy! No jumping! I'm still trying to train her not to jump," Chet says, pulling her by the collar and demanding she sit.

"No worries. How's your dad doing?" Chloe asks. "I see him driving in and out of the garage but never out and about in the neighborhood."

"He's busy at work lately. He has lots of clients at his new job. He really seems to like it. He's doing much better. I will try to get him to come over soon. I can't remember the last time he hung out with Fred."

"I'll tell Fred to reach out to him when he gets home later today. Maybe we can all get together for a Christmas cocktail later this evening," suggests Chloe.

"Do that," Chet says while taking the cake plate from Chloe's hands.

"Hope to see you both later," says Chloe genuinely.

"Me too," he says, staring at his sneakers and scratching his poorly grown goatee. Then he lifts his head to smile at Luna. He steps forward, closing the distance between them. His eyes fixate on her recently expanded breasts.

"Time to go." Chloe grabs Luna's arm. "See you soon."

"Wha—Mom!" Luna cries, not willing to leave so abruptly.

Goldy barks as they leave.

Later that evening, upon Harry's return from work, he enters with his uncle, George.

"Hi, Uncle George," Chet says. "Merry Christmas."

"Merry Christmas," he returns.

"Dad, Chloe, and Luna brought by the Christmas fruitcake for us. It's an Italian one. Looks tasty. Can we have a slice?"

"No, I don't want it," says Harry, waving his hand away.

"I'll have a slice," says Uncle George.

"You can bring home the entire cake. I don't need the neighborhood doting on me like an injured puppy. I'm fine. I don't need good luck or anyone bothering me. I'm doing just fine," Harry says, rubbing his hand where his pinky once was.

"Sorry, Dad. They are trying to do something nice, is all."

"I know. I'm sorry for the outburst—long day. We're going to Uncle George's tonight. We can bring the cake over there."

"Alright."

"No worries. I'll bring it over now," says Uncle George. "See you later." He delicately carries the cake out the door.

"See you later," says Chet.

Uncle George sets the cake on the passenger seat and pulls out of the driveway, gingerly making his way around the cul-de-sac.

A few minutes into the drive back home, he fails to notice a stop sign slightly obstructed by a hanging tree branch from last night's torrential thunderstorm. As he drives through it, he nearly hits a teenager walking his dog. He swerves onto the sidewalk, reaching for the fruitcake by instinct so it won't fall, strangely more concerned about the cake than his own well-being.

He wraps the car around one of the new streetlights the city installed a few weeks back. The airbag explodes, crushing his lungs and cracking his chest, a force too great for his eighty-five-year-old constitution. Death was instantaneous.

Chapter Twenty-One

Super Bowl Party
February 2, 2020
Holly

S uper Bowl 2020. This year could not possibly be the same without Harry and his entertaining commentary. Already, no one is very excited about the game without the Patriots and Brady, although most of the men are fans of Patrick Mahomes. Still, no Kansas City shirts are worn. Out of respect for the GOAT, the greatest of all time, we all wear our Brady shirts nevertheless.

"Today won't be the same without Harry," says Fred after sucking down his first of many Miller Lites.

"Well, go get him then. I'm sure he's home," suggests Chloe.

"Bradley will get him out. He can talk a dog off a meat wagon," I say proudly. "No one has the gift of gab quite like Bradley."

"Happy to oblige, my lady," he says with a formal bow.

"I'll go with you," offers Fred. "The game starts in fifteen minutes. Let's go."

"Alright then, me too," Harrington chimes in.

While the guys are out of the house, the ladies and I gather in the kitchen to open a few bottles of prosecco.

"I hope the guys can get him out of the house. It's been a full year without any real interaction, and after the incident with his uncle, I'm sure he could use friends right now." Chloe pops open the first bottle and pours the bubbles into four glasses.

"Four glasses? Is Gina coming?" asks Greta.

"She said she would be here for kickoff."

"Really? I'm impressed. I didn't think she followed football," I say, but nothing Gina does or doesn't do would surprise me. Then, as if on cue, Gina arrives.

"Hello, ladies," Gina calls out after slamming the front door loudly. Always a forceful entrance.

"Hey, girl, we were just about to make a toast. The guys are over at Harry's, trying to peel him away from his recliner," I explain.

"Terrible about his uncle's accident," says Gina as she reaches for a champagne glass.

"Indeed," murmurs Greta.

"Let's make a toast to Brady. You will always be in our thoughts and minds," says Chloe, and we clink and sip.

Just as the national anthem is about to begin, the guys walk in with Harry. Everyone rushes to the door for hugs.

"Pause the TV!" Chloe demands. "I don't want to miss Demi Lovato's rendition of the national anthem."

"You can't pause the Super Bowl, wifey! That's un-American," Fred yells defiantly to Chloe.

"Alright then, everyone sit. Love on Harry later. Sorry, Harry, big fan," Chloe says while ushering everyone to the couches. "Happy you came over, though."

"Thank you," says Harry.

"Hey, Harry, can—"

"SHHH!" Chloe cuts Fred off loudly, forcing us to watch Demi's performance in complete silence.

"Amazing!" I say, waiting a few extra moments after the final note to ensure I don't get slapped down by Chloe.

Gina gets up and meanders to the kitchen for more prosecco, and the rest of us ladies follow. "Did you notice Harry's hand?" she whispers loud enough for us to hear.

"Yes," I say. "I heard about his missing pinky, but do you know what actually happened to him?"

"No, but I have my suspicions," offers Greta.

"Do tell," says Chloe, putting down her champagne flute and staring at Greta, offering all her attention.

"Well, it was obviously a byproduct of his disappearance. Maybe he owed some people money, and they took his pinky as a form of payment." The three of us look at Greta like she may have lost her mind.

"Hmm," says Gina. "Interesting assumption."

"If you think about it, and hear me out—" Greta braces herself for an explanation with a sigh and a long pause, then continues, "—he disappears for four days. Maybe he's held captive. Then they take his finger as a warning not to mess with whoever took him. He comes home, speaks to no one as part of the pact with his captors, quits his job, and gets a new one because maybe the people who took him are people he pissed off during an acquisition. Or maybe he embezzled the money *from* an acquisition, and the people he worked for did this to him. The pinky . . . a trophy. He had to pay the piper, so to speak."

"Well, here we go. I guess we call you Velma for a reason. What does the rest of the Scooby-Doo gang think?" quips Gina.

"Very funny," says Greta. "Just a thought. And really, do I look like Velma?"

"Yup," says Gina, nodding.

"A very beautiful Velma," says Chloe.

"Cheers to Velma," I say, raising my glass.

We toast and sip.

"I think we need to be especially nice to Harry tonight," says Chloe. "Aside from his unfortunate circumstances, he lost his uncle on Christmas Eve."

"Yeah, about that," Greta says. "This is the second Christmas Eve death in the past two years. Maybe we should end this fruitcake exchange thing."

"So you're blaming Patty's and Harry's uncle's deaths on a fruitcake?" asks Gina, shaking her bangs away from her eyes.

"Well . . . no. Maybe . . . yes. I don't know. The fruitcake has some bad juju. Maybe this is some omen to stop this," Greta says, knowing how ridiculous this sounds. "In my defense," she says, "it sounded better in my head."

"That's ridiculous," says Gina. "So what we have here is a mob boss set loose in our neighborhood, snipping off fingers, and a haunted fruitcake?"

"Yeah, I know, sounds ludicrous," I agree.

Greta laughs nervously.

"What are you laughing at?" Harrington asks, approaching the kitchen.

"Oh, nothing, just a story about a mob boss looking for revenge," says Chloe.

"And a haunted fruitcake." Gina continues to giggle, and the rest of us chime in with more laughter.

"Touché," Greta says, giving up.

"What in the hell are you ladies talking about over there? The game started already," says Fred.

"Calm down, hubby," Chloe shouts back. "We don't care about this game. Brady is not playing. We don't care what happens."

I yell over, "Just tell us when it's halftime."

"Where are Luna and all the kids tonight?" asks Gina.

"She took Ana, Eva, Emmett, Rosco, and Rosie to the park, then driving them around the neighborhood in the golf cart. They should be back by halftime," says Chloe.

"I have to tell you, Chloe, I love it when Luna watches the kids. My kids ask so many random questions like, 'Mommy, why are there clouds? How big is the ocean? Where does my poop go when I flush?' Sometimes, I tell them to ask Luna. She is an expert on random facts. Watch out, college Jeopardy! She will be a formidable challenger one day."

"No doubt," Chloe agrees.

"She is also a brave little lady, entertaining our offspring," I say, reminding myself to tip Luna well. "Wrangling those kiddos will be no easy task. She may need to take tomorrow off from school to recover," I say, stating the obvious.

"Luna is great with the kids. She'll be fine," says Chloe.

"So you say . . . so you say." I worry, taking a large sip from my champagne glass.

Halftime delights us with Shakira and J.Lo's supercharged performance. The music and dancing are great, and I love that the performance includes two Spanish songs intertwined with some of their greatest hits. Nothing like adding a little Latin flair to the Super Bowl hosted by the Hard Rock Stadium in Miami Gardens. Five stars in my book. The men mostly enjoy the skin-colored leotards embellishing the performers' half-naked, gyrating bodies, but Harry still looks sullen, barely speaking.

The 49ers lead the Chiefs twenty to ten when the fourth quarter begins. The commentator says, "It's Mahomes. He's down, swallowed up with a sack."

Finally, Harry breaks his silence and says, you guessed it, "That's what she said: swallowed up with a sack."

We all laugh, and just like that, Harry's back!

Chapter Twenty-Two

The Tall Lady
December 8, 2022
Dr. Davis

I awaken to the sun glistening through the window just out of reach. Dust particles linger and move about in slow motion, naked to the human eye outside the ray of sun beaming toward me. Nature's beauty soothes my soul. The sunlight offers hope for a better day and a new beginning, even in these horrific circumstances.

I cast my mind back to my elementary school days, staring out the classroom window, enjoying the same, but different, dust particles dancing around in the sunlight. It's funny how you instinctively return to the places you feel most comfortable in turmoil.

If only anyone would walk past my window and peer in to find me. I know the likelihood of this is slim. Why is the window not blacked out for wandering, nosy eyes? This is such a flaw in their plan. But I also know that no one ever gets close to the Hudson house. The women who live here are creepy. There are rumors in the neighborhood, which I picked up from the local housewives, that these ladies are strange and sinister, but for the love of God, I can no longer remember their backstory. I tend to block out all the neighborhood gossip and petty grievances among the residents. Now, I wish that I had paid closer attention.

At this point of the day, on a typical day, I would have gotten up and drunk at least one cup of coffee, and I would be in the middle of a three-mile walk before twenty minutes of intense weight training in my garage, then making my rounds at the hospital.

Today, the steel door creaks open, and a woman steps in. My eyes are still adjusting, and I can tell she is tall, slender, and smells clean, like a combination of fresh-cut flowers and cotton linens with hints of coconut and strawberries. Her beauty and grace make me feel unclean, both physically and emotionally.

She walks in slowly without saying a word. She sits beside me on the floor. She stares along with me toward the ray of light that enters through the window in the basement. I should say something, anything, but I find myself tongue-tied in my tiredness and confusion. I allow myself a moment to enjoy her lovely fragrance. It's been a long time since my nasal passages have encountered such an explosion of joy.

We sit silently for a few minutes. Then she finally turns her head toward me and speaks.

"How are you doing?" she asks, genuinely interested in my well-being.

Her eyes—a penetrating, intelligent blue momentarily set me at ease. I feel her breath against my cheek. Peppermint.

"I've been better," I admit—an obvious response.

"Thank you for confessing to your role in the death of your girlfriend's husband. That must have been difficult for you. The most important part of recovery is owning your past and acknowledging all your mistakes."

She pauses a few moments, then continues. "Let's talk about the drug addicts and the vagrants."

She looks disappointed and sad as if she could cry at any moment. I can sense her hidden reservoir of pain.

"I've been told you allowed two drug addicts to die and a homeless man who came through the ER convulsing. You could have stepped in to push fluids and lifesaving meds, but you allowed them to perish under your watch instead. I also know about the few cancer patients you helped administer deadly doses of morphine to end their lives. For this I pass, or shall I say, *we* pass no judgment."

"Who are *we*?" I ask quietly, trying not to upset her.

"Never you mind."

"Who are you?"

"I can't say right now. But I have been where you are. Let's just leave it at that for now."

I have so many questions, but I'm paralyzed now, and the questions I want to ask don't come. Instead, I ask, "What comes next?"

"Soon, you will be given stationery and envelopes, many of them. You will write letters asking forgiveness from those who perished under your care and supervision. Upon your departure, you will bury these letters by their graves. These letters are not for the dead but rather a form of penance as you take responsibility for their deaths. You will also write a letter to each of their families. When the time is right, we will mail them just before you're released."

"Will that be soon?" I need to know. I have to know. I'm afraid of the response.

"Yes, soon." She takes my hands in hers and stares deeply into my eyes, then says, "I am rooting for you, Dr. Davis. You can change your path and make great changes to and for this community. The goal here is that you can work your way back to something solid, stable, and rewarding in your life."

She pushes herself up from the floor, opens the metal door, and slams it shut without looking back.

My heart swells—my stomach flutters. I don't want to feel any emotion for her. I feel the heat in my cheeks. I'm fragile right now like I could shatter into a million pieces at any moment. I wish she hadn't left so soon.

The door reopens within a few minutes of her departure, and a tray slides toward me with spaghetti and meatballs, water, stationery, envelopes, and a pen. Time to get to work.

Chapter Twenty-Three

Twins
October 1993
Judge Hudson

After ten years toiling away as a public defender, AJ ran for and won the elected office of circuit court judge.

At home, there was even better news. After many years of trying to conceive children, fraternal twin girls were born at thirty-six weeks. One infant weighed a hefty nine pounds, the other five pounds, two ounces.

Shortly after they were born, the OB nurse said, trying to add a bit of light commentary after a long and arduous delivery, "These two sure are feisty. Good luck with these hellions."

Esther had always imagined children of her own would be far easier than raising other people's broken children. She was wrong. Children enter the world with their unique personalities, one different from another. While you can advise and mentor a child in the right direction, each has their own temperament, personality traits, predispositions, abilities, and imperfections given to them at birth that manifest over time.

Ma slipped away in her sleep the same day the twins were born. Such is the circle of life. As souls leave the earth, others enter. The babies were both named after Ma. The firstborn, the larger twin, they called Trudy, and the other, smaller twin, they named after Ma's middle name, Leigh.

Esther was devastated by Ma's death. After hearing the news, she was so distraught she couldn't muster the will to feed or hold the children. At her bedside in the hospital, AJ tried to comfort her.

"It's going to be alright. Ma drifted off in her sleep peacefully. She would have loved to be here for you, Esther, but I promise, although I could never take her place, I will be here for you to help raise our children. I love you, and I love our family."

"The twins are not a gift from God. I'm cursed. They're doomed. They're ugly, marked by sin. Even the nurse said they were hellions."

"I am sure the nurse didn't mean hellions in the way you think she did."

Esther looked past him toward the door like she was expecting a visit from someone else. She continued in a mumble and went on about how one of the infants was too big and had a rash on her belly and a misshapen head, while the other had ugly moles on her face.

"Honey," AJ tried to reassure her, "babies look a bit unpleasant when born. They've just undergone a lot of trauma. Birth is traumatic but also a miracle."

"They're hideous. I don't want them," she insisted.

"Esther, I'm sure you don't mean that. You love children. We've already fostered so many, and you love them all."

Esther handed AJ a folded letter she had hidden under her pillow. It read:

Dear Esther,
Due to your life choices, you are
destined for a life of pain and unhappiness.
Since you turned your back on the
marriage to your future husband, Pastor
James, God's disciple of our Lord and
Savior, your remaining life on this Earth
will be filled with sadness and sorrow.
Your life trajectory will only lead you to
the gates of Hell. Should you reconsider
choosing to excommunicate from the
community, you know where to find us.
—Mom and Dad

What parents would write such a letter? Say such things? AJ couldn't imagine the pain Esther was feeling. It would take an entire lifetime to undo the pain she had undergone in her young life in the cult she was raised in. Esther had been hit with so many circumstances all at once. It was unfair. The death of Ma, the letter from her parents, and the birth of the twins. Her postpartum depression ran so deep that she spent a week in bed, refusing to eat or talk to anyone.

When she finally mustered enough courage to get out of bed, she ambled her way to the bathroom, where she snatched a razor blade from the medicine cabinet behind the bathroom mirror. Esther sat on the bathroom floor and sliced her skin with small but deep cuts between each toe on both feet. She watched the blood trickle along the white ceramic tiles. She momentarily enjoyed the temporary relief from her sadness and the beautiful art her blood designed along the shiny tiles and grout lines. She then dipped her feet into a tub of rubbing alcohol. The pain embraced her like a warm, fuzzy blanket. This was the only coping mechanism that quenched the overwhelming emotions she found difficult to speak about or control. Childhood memories flood back to her. She was reminded of all the times in her childhood when she needed to expel her suffering and painful emotions with the distraction of a razor blade and then punish her behavior with rubbing alcohol.

AJ found Esther by the front door with a packed suitcase two weeks after bringing the twins home.

"Where are you going?"

"I'm checking myself into the hospital for psychiatric care. I need this, AJ. Please let me do this. It's for my sanity."

"Alright, I'll do this for you because I love you, and I need you to snap out of whatever torment you are putting yourself through."

With his ma dead and his wife in rehab, AJ hired round-the-clock care to help raise the twins until Esther was well enough to come home. The other children and teenagers they fostered at the time helped as much as could be expected while not at school or work.

When Esther returned five months later, she wasn't quite the same. She never did find a way to bond with the girls. She stayed clear of them entirely. She insisted the twins were a punishment from God for leaving her community and that the girls were sent to punish both of them, their family, and their home. She believed that they possessed only the worst qualities of her character.

Esther instead focused her love and attention on the foster children. She ensured they got good grades in school, jobs in the community and dated only those with good intentions.

Over the following years, the rehabilitation room was only used for the twins but never for more than a few days at a time. AJ never stepped in the way of her discipline. He worked for such long hours in those days, distracted and caught up in his career that he turned a blind eye, something he would come to regret.

When the twins turned twelve, Esther claimed both girls were too challenging to handle. Even days holed up in the rehabilitation room didn't seem to heal or correct certain unpleasant tendencies.

One summer morning, when Leigh was seven years old, Esther caught her maiming a lizard. She was poking a safety pin through its skin.

"Mommy, I just want to see if lizards have thick skin like their ancestors, the dinosaurs," she explained.

But it wasn't the explanation that concerned Esther. It was the terrifying, hair-raising, crooked smile she possessed while saying it. In the years that passed, Esther found her tormenting Japanese beetles in the yard by pulling off their legs and once found her coaxing a squirrel into eating rat poison pellets that she dunked in peanut butter. But when Esther found a shoebox full of rat tails under Leigh's bed, she decided Leigh's days at home with them were numbered.

Trudy, on the other hand, was a kinder, gentler soul. She had many friends at school, but because of her size, she often got into trouble defending her little sister. She was known to break a nose or two along the way when anyone made fun of the moles on her sister's face.

Esther decided to send them both off to her home state of Utah. So, in the fall of 2005, Esther enrolled the girls in the Diamond Ranch Academy for troubled teens. They could visit only for Christmas and one week over summer vacation.

"Are you sure you want to do this?" AJ pleaded with Esther to reconsider. "You harbor quite a bit of resentment and trauma from your days in Utah. Are you sure that you want to do this to our kids?"

"Different circumstances. I was being forced to marry the pastor in my church, who already had, um, I don't know . . . eight, maybe ten other wives. This school is specially designed for troubled teens."

"I wouldn't say our kids are troubled, exactly. I've seen far worse."

"Seriously?" Esther shrugged and let out a long sigh filled with exasperation. "You've seen the box of rat tails under Leigh's bed. You've repeatedly been in the principal's office for Trudy's temper and fighting on school grounds. These girls need help."

"Alright, alright. I'll agree to whatever you wish. I don't want any battles."

Before the girls left home for school, Esther gifted each daughter a Rubik's Cube and an inspirational book, *The Power of Now,* by Eckhart Tolle. "For your journey…one will help pass the time, and one will enlighten the mind."

Chapter Twenty-Four

Peeping Toms
March 2020
Holly

I 'm sure everyone can remember where they were when the local morning newscasters delivered the news that we were going into lockdown in March 2020 due to COVID-19. It was expected, however. Since January, most people have known this flu-like virus was spreading rapidly worldwide.

Just last week, Bradley began working from home. His talent searches will be moved entirely online until further notice. That made me incredibly happy. Having him home like a real family for a while will be great. And I am definitely going to need the help with the kids during lockdown. Keeping my kiddos entertained and up-to-date on their schoolwork will be a formidable challenge. The very first thing I did that morning was ask Francesca to move in. She has lived alone since her mom passed away last year.

My cell phone rings the morning of lockdown immediately following the news.

"Hey, Gina," I say, excited to hear from her.

"Are you going to be okay?" she asks.

"What do you mean?"

"Well, we may be in lockdown for a while. Will you be able to cope with the kids? Is Bradley going to continue to work from home?"

"Yeah, I think I'll be alright. Francesca has moved in, and Bradley is already working from home."

"Oh, great. I was worried about you."

"Thank you for thinking of me. What about you? I'm sure not much will change for you, but it will get lonely over there all alone."

"Yeah, I know, but I have an idea. Let's bring our yoga mats to the sidewalk every morning, six feet apart, of course, with our coffees, spend some girl time chatting, then let's stream a yoga or Peloton exercise class to keep our sanity."

"Great idea! Yes!"

So, for the next few months, the ladies and I get together in the mornings for coffee chat and yoga. The guys get together a few evenings a week with their coolers, folding chairs, and Fred's portable TV. Every Friday, we meet with our spouses for happy hour in the cul-de-sac at 6:00 p.m. To be honest, this is not so bad. Francesca cooks and cleans, while Bradley helps me with the kids' schoolwork in the early morning hours before I meet with the ladies. Before long, restaurants reopen, and we can get away if we wear our masks.

With Bradley home and helping with the kids and Francesca taking care of the house, I decide it's time to take care of *me* for a change. Taking advice from my friends, I decide to dye my hair blonde, like I had during my short-lived music career.

Since salons are closed, Gina suggests a color specialist she worked with while modeling. We chat over Zoom, and my first words are, "Please pick a shade of blonde with a spectacular name." My choices are Extreme, Supreme, or Hyper Platinum—nothing too fancy. I settle on Hyper Platinum. I think that best suits my personality.

She mails the color packet and solution to me, and a few days later, I am a whole new woman. I know it's just hair color, but suddenly I feel sexier and, surprisingly, invincible. I'm sure there is no science to prove this, but it sparked my creativity.

After breakfast and sidewalk class with the ladies, I started writing again. Mostly just the lyrics—the music usually comes later, and Bradley is a big help in that respect. He has an excellent ear for melody.

With little to do in the evenings besides watching TV, Greta and I decide to prowl around the neighborhood, taking long walks once the kids are in bed to help unwind from the day. What is unexpected is that we became rather nosy. In our defense, we're bored. I think we became—well, the accurate term, I believe, is Peeping Toms. The things you can discover about a person by peering in the windows as you walk past are undeniably addicting.

Walking alongside my property line to my backyard one evening, we realize we can peer directly into Gina's studio. This is where the magic happens, I presume. The place she photographs her feet. But what is interesting is that the room is lined with shelves filled with trophies from her beauty pageant days—so many of them.

One day, when Greta and I walk past her studio window, Gina rests her feet inside a large spaghetti platter with a few meatballs and garlic rolls.

"Give me a boost," I say.

Greta intertwines her fingers, and I put my foot inside her hands as she pushes me to see better. I tap on the window and wave.

Gina flinches, turns suddenly, smiles, and yells, "You nearly gave me a heart attack! I can't get up right now. Call you in a bit." Then I boost Greta, and she knocks and waves.

Gina later texts us the finished photo. It's titled *Dinner: Toe-tally Italian.*

Most evenings, the Hudson house goes dark around 8:00 p.m. Some evenings, loud music plays. Occasionally, a large black SUV pulls up, drives into the garage, and leaves minutes later. Very strange.

Greta wants to peek in their windows, but they have so much surveillance that it would be impossible to peer inside undetected.

One evening, when the weather is cool and the windows open, we can hear the goings-on in everyone's homes as we walk past.

Harry suggests to Chet that he call some girl. "What are you afraid of? I'm sure she likes you."

When we approach Chloe's house, we hear a bloodcurdling scream. It sounds like Luna. She's yelling, "Mom, Mommm, make it stop! Make it stop!"

So, of course, we rush to the door, knocking loudly, and then we hear Luna say, "I don't want to look at that. Come over here and get your husband! Mom, it's awful. Hurry! Tell him to cover himself. This is obscene."

"Chloe, open up! Is everything alright?" We both continue banging on the door.

Chloe finally answers, laughing.

"Is everything alright?" I ask. "What's so funny? We heard screaming."

"Come on in," she says.

Upon entering the living room, it is clear what all the commotion was about. Fred is on the Peloton bike, half-naked, wearing only ill-fitting bike shorts, no shirt, belly hanging way over. Quite a sight to see, and from now on, I will never be able to unsee this moment. Even funnier, a half-empty bottle of Miller Lite sits where a water bottle is usually placed.

Fred, not embarrassed at all, says, "Hey, ladies, I know, I know . . . you're both eager for some eye candy. Stay a while. I've got thirty minutes left of my class with Cody Rigsby."

"Um," I say, and I am left with a loss of words.

"If you want to follow me on Peloton, my handle is fat Freddy, all one word with two y's." Then he starts belting out the words to the Britney Spears song "Baby One More Time" at the top of his lungs, along with Cody. To be honest, he has a pretty nice voice.

"I'm so sorry. I didn't mean to alarm anyone," says Luna. "My dad is so embarrassing. He scared me. That's why I screamed. I heard grunting coming from the living room. I didn't expect to find my dad naked, drunk, and groaning on the exercise bike."

Chloe is still laughing.

But that wasn't the end of that. Eager to punish us for the intrusion, Fred stages pranks when we pass the bay window in the evenings. One night, he hangs from a noose, tongue hanging out, in the window as we walk past, and another time, he sits in the window, bloodied and playing dead, with a bloody axe leaning against the window frame.

"Very funny, Fred," we call out. "Very funny!" It serves us right for snooping, I suppose.

Chapter Twenty-Five

The Rubik's Cube and the Book
December 9, 2022
Dr. Davis

L etters are written, folded, and placed gently in each envelope, awaiting pickup by my captors. I place them behind my pillow. Rain falls angrily against the only window that keeps me imprisoned, separating me from the outside world. Today, I feel good. Lighter, dare I say? Enlightened, if I must be honest with myself. Something is to be noted about confessing indiscretions that eat at your soul. Certain sins slowly eat you alive from the inside out until you can one day forgive yourself. While I should be angry, scared, and consumed by trying to find ways to escape, I feel at peace oddly. I'm quietly optimistic about my release.

The overhead lights flicker at eight this morning, and the door clamors open. Two women argue outside the door. I hear only "Soon" and "Stick with the plan."

My eyes are drawn to a flash of movement beyond the door, beyond the women. I hear a scream. I can hear my breathing, short, shallow breaths, fear creeping in. Then, before the tall woman enters the room, another cry comes from elsewhere in the basement. Are there other prisoners? The voices . . . they sound male. Could there have been other people down here with me all along? Could they hear me if I yell? What could they have done to find themselves in this same situation?

The tall lady walks unsteadily toward me. She hands me a tray of food. Today, the menu consists of oatmeal, a banana, and a bowl of fried chicken. I place the tray on my bed, reach behind my pillow, and hand her the letters.

"Here you go," I say.

"How do you feel?" she asks.

"I'm alright. Strangely, I feel pretty good after writing the letters."

"That's not strange at all," she says, sitting beside me on the bed.

She trusts me. She believes that I trust her. I could easily attack her right now, strangle her. I'm clearly stronger. She doesn't seem worried.

She puts her hand on my knee and whispers in my ear, "I'm proud of you."

I'm immediately aroused by her touch, her fragrance, her attention. Every square inch of my skin tingles with her touch. Her scent is intoxicating. She smells like coconut and strawberries. She's sitting so close that I can tell the coconut scent is from her lotion and strawberry from shampoo. I can only bathe in her delightful aroma for a few moments before my thoughts bring me back to my own reality, and I become hypersensitive to my pungent odor. Now I'm embarrassed. I wish we could have met under different circumstances. I have read about people who become enamored by their captors. Stockholm syndrome, I think they call it. I try to snap myself out of this feeling. Her fragrance mocks my grief. But this moment is special, and I intend to enjoy it.

"I was once where you are. I understand what you are going through." Her hand is caressing my leg more aggressively.

"Imagine your entire life as a maze from a childhood activity book." She pauses a moment for my imagination to kick in. "Every turn you take, right, left, or straight ahead, was a choice you made."

"Alright," I say, playing along. I'm just delighted to be in her presence having her attention right now.

"Close your eyes."

" Alright," I oblige.

"Now that you have reached the exit, imagine you could go back and change some of your life choices. Would you?"

"Yes."

"I will leave you with this thought. Dr. Davis, We are doing important work here, and you are doing very well."

We sit in silence for a few moments, then she stands. She walks toward the door, knocks a few times, and another woman answers. That woman hands her two items. She turns back around, smiling, and walks back toward me.

"This is for you," she says, handing me a book and a toy.

"Thank you," I say, inspecting the items. A Rubik's Cube and a book by Eckhart Tolle titled *The Power of Now*. She turns and walks toward the door. Her scent lingers. I wish once again that she would stay longer.

"I'll be back in a few days, after you receive your penance," she says flatly, her voice colder.

"I'll give you money, anything you want. Just let me go home." I don't know why I blurted that out. Desperation makes you do strange things.

"What got you here won't get you there, Dr. Davis. You've got to do the work."

"I just want to go home," I plead.

"In due time, Dr. Davis. In due time."

I look over the items in my hands again, confused by it all, when she suggests, "One will help pass the time, and one will enlighten the mind."

The door slams shut.

"Yes, ma'am," I mutter to myself.

Sad, lonely, and afraid, I already miss her.

Chapter Twenty-Six

The New Neighbor
April 2020
Holly

Greta chose a lower body class on her Peloton app for this morning's sidewalk class. Chase, the instructor, has us start with twenty squats. Chloe, Gina, and I start the squat series, but Greta stands in place.

"What's wrong?" I ask.

"Um, I can't do squats in public."

"What?"

"Why?"

"Since when?"

We all follow up with our own questions.

"Well, squats make me fart, um, loudly, and, well, so I don't do them in public anymore." Greta's face is flustered, and she starts to laugh.

Now we're all laughing so hard that Greta has to pause the class.

"I don't believe you," snipes Gina. "Prove it."

Greta does her squat; sure enough, a short but thunderous fart escapes from her booty.

Through the mist of laughter, Gina says, "No more boom boom in the zoom zoom for you, girlfriend. Your booty box has had enough. The air escaping is probably because it's all stretched out."

More laughter ensues.

"I am quite sure that's not the problem I'm having," Greta insists.

"So this is *not* an adverse effect of dancing the chocolate cha-cha?" Gina banters back.

"No! I don't do that," says Greta defiantly, but then she cracks, barely able to keep her face from laughter. "Well, if I *did* do that, which I definitely *did not*, my defense would be, what else is there to do at home during Covid than Netflix and chill?"

"Netflix, chill, and mashing brownies, maybe?" Gina proposes. "And what do *you* think about all of this, Chloe?"

Chloe, thrown off balance by the question, answers, "Um, well, maybe drinking more water and less high-fiber foods could help? I think passing gas during rigorous exercise is common. Isn't it? Anyway, how about we pick a new class to take?"

We agree to take a twenty-minute core routine class on the mat, concentrating on our tummies. But, for the remainder of the morning, none of us can keep a straight face.

Shortly after the class ends, a giant moving truck enters the cul-de-sac and stops in front of Patty's old house. A red Ferrari follows behind, and a strange looking man with bright red hair and a seersucker suit emerges. I already know this guy is going to be a douche.

"Someone needs to tell him a redhead has no business driving a red car," offers Gina. "And seersucker? Really? Did he just get back from the Kentucky Derby?"

"It won't be me," says Greta. "He looks too much like many of the blowhards I work with in my office. No, thank you."

"Blowhard?" Maybe try that, Greta, and give your butt a break." Gina laughs. She's really on a roll with her jokes this morning. Strangely, we're all entertained by Gina's snide remarks. These days, since concerts, movies, and music festivals are canceled until no one knows when, Gina is our best avenue for amusement.

"Well, if this new neighbor misbehaves, we can always deliver a fruitcake. Problem solved," I say.

"Good idea," says Gina. "I heard from the new HOA lady that he's renting Patty's house until her children settle their fight over the estate."

The new guy looks our way and blows a kiss in our direction. We all look at each other wide-eyed until Gina says, "Did he just kiss us?"

I mutter quietly, "*Come pinga!*"

"What does that mean?" Chloe asks timidly.

"It's bad. Look it up later." I shy away from the answer.

"It means, what a dick!"

I'm not surprised Gina would blurt that out for the entire neighborhood to hear.

We continue watching the new guy move in and boss the movers around while we stretch.

"Ladies, let's not snoop so obviously. Meet up for drinks later in the cul-de-sac?" I suggest.

"Sure," says Chloe, rolling up her exercise mat.

"I know what you'll be doing until then," I say to Greta with a wink.

"Don't be an ass, Holly."

"Not *your* ass. No, thank you," I say, and we all giggle at her expense.

Chapter Twenty-Seven

The House of Refuge
May 2020
Holly

T he doorbell rings shortly after Charlie collects the kids to bring to school.

"Hello. What are you doing right now?" asks Gina.

"Um, cleaning the kitchen. The kids just left. Come on in."

"Oh good gravy, what happened in here? The house smells like a hockey locker room."

"We call it Eau de Emmett with a hint of Rosco. Raising boys is a smelly job," I say with a little shrug.

"You should get those little air freshener packet doohickeys. You know, the ones they use in the gyms? Put them right behind the vent grates."

"Good idea. I'll look later on Amazon. I'm sure they sell something like that."

"Amazon sells everything."

"Follow me into the kitchen. Let me clean up the breakfast table. My little mess-makers left me a doozy today. Bradley is on an important conference call in the office. So breakfast with the kids was all on me. Sorry for the disarray."

"Seriously, Holly, there are Froot Loops all over the floor, the table . . . and hey, look at that," she says, pointing to the ceiling. "This is a disaster zone."

"Oh shit, I bet that's what they were giggling about this morning. Ugh. They must have been flicking Froot Loops with their spoons to see if they could get those mini sugar circles to stick. Let me get a broom."

"Give *me* the broom," Gina offers. "I'm taller. It'll be easier for me to scrape these off the twelve-foot ceilings with the broom if I do it."

"I'm sorry, I'm outnumbered around here, you know. I leave them for just a few minutes, and no telling what I'll find when I return."

As Gina brushes the Froot Loops off the ceiling, a few fall to the floor. One bounces off the cabinets and lands back into one of the cereal bowls.

"Wish I caught that one on video. Bet it would go viral."

Gina laughs, then asks, "Hey, how do you feel about heading out to the beach today for a walk along the shore by the House of Refuge?"

"Sure. I mean, I don't know where or what the House of Refuge is, but a walk along the beach sounds great right about now."

"The House of Refuge is the museum you pass before entering the neighborhood. It's the last standing structure in Florida for shipwreck survivors. It's great to visit after a wicked storm like the one that hit us last night. The tide brings in the most beautiful shells along the shoreline after a big storm," Gina explains. "As angry waves crash along the seaboard, large colorful shells from deep within the Atlantic find their way to shore. Nature's wrath can be swift and violent but, at the same time, leave behind lovely trinkets for us to enjoy. So let's go."

"So what I hear you saying is that you want to collect some shells for your next photo shoot with your feet?"

"Yes, exactly." She smiles. "Go put on your bathing suit, get your beach bag, and let's go have some fun."

As we head out the door, Bradley rushes out of the office in despair. "Help!" he cries. "My conference call starts in five minutes, and I can't push these square buttons through the round holes in my shirt. Who invented this? It's stupid."

"I'm going to guess a woman. Probably as a form of payback for all the years men designed pantyhose, ill-fitting, itchy bras, runway dresses only in size six, and grandma panties. Serves you right," I tell him as I button him up.

"Nice shirt, though." Gina winks at Bradley. "Happy Zooming."

"Have a great time, ladies," Bradley says, whispering in my ear, "Hurry home, sugar britches."

"Sugar britches? Really? Disgusting," Gina says, mimicking a gag reflex, then rolling her eyes.

"Disgusting? That's just rich from the woman who lathers her feet with festive culinary cuisine. He loves me, that's all. He's hardly home, so when he is, we have to make up for all that lost time in bed. This Covid lockdown has been great for us. Sugar britches is our code for— Let's do it."

"Repulsive. Too much information. And also, good for you. I'm jealous. Bradley is the perfect husband. He spends most of the time out of your hair but shows up just when you need him."

"It was difficult when the kids were small, but now that they're older, I welcome the time alone when he travels. That's more time I can spend with you and the girls."

"Friendship makes the dream work."

"That's what they say . . ."

We arrive at the beach shortly after 8:00 a.m. The calm and bright blue ocean today reflects the beauty of a clear sapphire sky. The beach is already full of shell seekers and treasure hunters roaming around the shoreline with their beach bags and metal detectors.

"My older siblings used to take me here when I was a kid. There's no place like it after a storm. All the locals venture here looking for long-lost treasure the sea gifts back to humanity."

The sun peeks through the clouds, and miles of seashore are covered with pretty new seashells and plenty of sea glass. Nature's wrath never looks so beautiful as Hutchinson Island beaches this morning.

"Oh no," says Gina. "There's Willa. The neighborhood sucker."

"Sucker?"

"Yeah, she sucks the life out of every conversation."

"I met her at the park with the kids before," I say. "She told me about the teenager in the neighborhood that went missing a few years back. Then she said he turned his life around."

"Well, she's a bit batty," says Gina, making the universal crazy sign with her pointer finger over her right ear.

"Hey, ladies," Willa yells, waving an arm above her head. Her gray hair is pulled back in a bun under a long-billed visor with oversized sunglasses to keep the sun from scorching her face. She's holding a trash picker in her hand, strolling over to us through the sand and shells.

"Hey, Willa," says Gina. "How are you?" A nicety she offers but doesn't care to know the answer to.

"Beautiful shells this morning, right?" I say while leaning over to collect a few pretty pink shells and place them into my beach bag.

"You're the one with all the kids. Holly, right?"

"Yes, we met at the park once."

"Yes, I remember."

"I don't think we've ever had anyone in the neighborhood with so many kids."

"Really?"

"You don't allow your kids to watch those blasphemous animated movies, do you? Like *Shrek*? You know, all that sexual innuendo in those films is a disgrace."

"Here we go," whispers Gina for only me to hear.

Secretly, I love that about modern-day animated movies. There is something to enjoy for all ages. The innuendo goes over the heads of the little ones and lands perfectly amongst the adults. But I don't engage. I know too well that you can't talk butterfly to caterpillar people.

"Or maybe *Harry Potter*," she continues, "which is also blasphemy. That story is the work of the Devil, delighting children with witchcraft. So disturbing."

Gina turns to me and mouths the word *sucker*.

I nod and say to Willa, "Of course, I only choose movies with good moral value."

I look at Gina and shrug while Willa looks down and spikes a plastic water bottle with her picker.

"Kids today trashing the beach makes me angry," Willa continues complaining.

"I can't imagine," Gina whispers to me.

"And one other thing. This fruitcake thing you are doing in your cul-de-sac. The Devil has a hand in that as well."

"What? Why do you say that?" asks Gina.

"Strange things have been happening around the neighborhood. Teenagers have gone missing. Men have gone missing. I have lived in this neighborhood for twenty years. These disappearances are not new. Now, people are dying by fruitcake on Christmas. This is not a coincidence. It's all connected."

"What do the disappearances have to do with fruitcake? How many people disappeared?"

"Don't you ladies know that our neighborhood is cursed?"

"Cursed?" We both say in unison.

"Your generation of Botox and butt lifts leaves you oblivious! I don't know why I even bother." She takes a deep breath, then starts in again. "Our neighborhood used to be called the Seminole Shores, once covered in beautiful orange groves. Anyway, it was home to Native Americans. The Seminoles would travel from Indiantown to our neighborhood for a few months of the year to trade with folks from Stuart. They would join the Ais and Jaega tribes that were already settled here. Doesn't anyone read history books anymore? Those stupid phones you ladies covet scramble your minds. The property was sold from beneath them or stolen. No one knows the full details, but the Seminoles never returned. All three tribes just disappeared from the area. Legend has it that this land is cursed."

"So what does that have to do with fruitcake?" I ask.

"One of the items the Native Americans traded was an American Indian Christmas cake. It was popular because it was made with hard-to-find hazelnuts, with dates and thick goat milk adding additional flavor. Come by the park sometime. Florida is steeped in tradition for abusing the natives. I have plenty of stories."

"Alright, Willa," I say. "It was nice seeing you. Gina and I are here to collect a few shells. We don't have much time. We've got to move along. I hope to run into you in the park soon. I'd love to hear more about haunted Laguna Palms," I say facetiously.

Willa cocks her head and follows us with a glaring, distrustful look in her eyes as we walk away. She yells off in our direction, "Not haunted . . . cursed."

"Batshit crazy, that lady."

"Mm-hmm," I agree, "or as my Cuban dad would say, '*Vieja loca.*' "

"Huh?"

"Crazy witch," I clarify, which catches a chuckle from Gina.

My yoga instructor once said: "You shouldn't always surround yourself with like-minded people. You should embrace opposing ideas. It's the only way to grow." For sure, she wasn't talking about Willa.

About an hour later, and both of our beach bags full of shells, Gina suggests we stop at Jan's Place in Jensen Beach for a late breakfast. I have never witnessed anyone devour chocolate chip pancakes the way Gina enjoys them—not a morsel left. I *want* to eat like a supermodel, allowing myself to eat dessert for breakfast, but, to be honest, a mere mortal like me can't possibly take in three thousand calories the same way her giant, super-tall body can consume such a fabulous feast.

After breakfast, pulling into my driveway, we discover Chloe chatting with both Hudson sisters in front of her house.

"They seem pretty friendly," says Gina sarcastically, staring off in their direction.

"Chloe is friendly to everyone," I tell her.

"What on earth could they be talking about? What could they possibly have in common? Is Chloe laughing? Weird." Gina sets the car in park and opens her door aggressively.

Chloe whips her head around in our direction, waves, smiles, offers some barely audible goodbye to the sisters, and off she goes, eyes lowered, head down, up the stairs, and into her house.

I collect my things from Gina's car, and we lock eyes. We both shrug, and at the same time, we say, "Weird."

Chapter Twenty-Eight

A Life Assessment
December 11, 2022
Dr. Davis

T he Rubik's Cube didn't survive the first night. I slammed it against the furthest wall in the basement in frustration. I was able to collect all the green squares to one side entirely, then got aggravated, threw it in a fit of rage, and now I can't reach it. It mocks me from the other side of the room. A stark reminder of my temper. Something I promise to turn around as soon as I'm released.

As I assess my life, I keep returning to what the tall lady told me. "I was once where you are. I understand what you're going through." What did she mean by that? What had she gone through? What did *she* have to confess? She seems so sweet, so kind. Could there be something real between us? I can't wait to see her again.

I spent the next two days reading Eckhart Tolle's book. The central theme from this book that most resonates with me is that joy, real joy, emanates from within. The present moment is all you ever have. The past disappears, the future hasn't happened, and every moment should be embraced and enjoyed today. The book teaches that I must surrender to the moment I find myself, focus on all I have to be thankful for, and commit to ways in which I can steer my life in a positive direction.

I should be thankful for my successful career, my home, and my good health. To be honest, I feel lonely . . . empty inside. I have not had one truly meaningful relationship in my life. I work seventeen-hour days, five or six days a week. I have superficial friends and shallow women in my life.

Tall Lady is correct. Re-examining my life is long overdue. But when I look at my life, I can't help but feel an overwhelming sadness. Enlightenment, the book explains, is simply the end of suffering. It's time for me to stop suffering. When I get out of here, everything will be different. This is my promise to myself in the wee hours before Tall Lady brings me my penance.

I'll join Orangetheory or F45, play racquetball at the fitness center, or do anything to meet people. I'll be nicer to my neighbors and colleagues, be more charitable, and help kids in need. I will most definitely be a better doctor, living up to the Hippocratic oath I promised to uphold. "In illness, one should keep two things in mind: to be useful and cause no harm." I'll mentor a few interns.

Maybe even spend a year or two overseas with the Doctors Without Borders organization. I'll go to church. Well . . . let's not overpromise.

I smile, proud of my ambitions. I'm making so many promises to myself as I sit here with my life in the hands of these women. Soon, I am promised release. I can do this. I just need to hang in there for a few more days.

Chapter Twenty-Nine

The Hudson House Rehabilitation Center
September 2015
Judge Hudson

AJ was terrible at heart-to-heart talks. Too painful. For that reason, Esther and he never spoke about her childhood. Ever. He figured if they never talked about it, it would somehow dissolve itself from existence. He knew this was unrealistic. AJ dealt with broken families and unhealthy relationships every day in the courtroom with regard to children, so he should know better. But at home, he was too afraid to bring up the past. He was honestly scared of what might unravel. So, he only spoke about the present and their hopes and dreams for the future.

However, he suggested she speak with a therapist from time to time over the years when sadness kicked in, like clockwork, each year around Ma's death, which is also the birthday of the twins, and the holidays. She had always refused to speak to a stranger. She and Ma had a great relationship that hoped to help heal the broken places within her heart and leave her past behind. But it wasn't until Ma's death, when

Esther entered rehab, that she spoke with a licensed therapist about her upbringing.

While she did not wholly abolish her demons with the family therapist in rehab, she embraced a few coping skills to come to terms with her childhood. But she never did find a loving place in her heart for her daughters.

When she came home, the nanny agreed to move in permanently to help raise the girls. On the weekends, AJ took the girls on outings to the beach, the movies, Disney parks, and camping along the Peace River in north Florida. While he and the girls created a special bond, Esther and the girls never did.

When the twins left for boarding school, Esther's happiness was apparent. It was as if a dark cloud had suddenly lifted, and she felt joy in all she did. She sang while doing daily chores around the house, hugged the foster kids more often, and jumped into AJ's arms when he returned home in the evenings. He never discussed the twins with her while they were away. He did keep in touch with the girls by phone and mail and sent weekly care packages.

All was well until the girls came home permanently in the fall of 2015 after graduating from Diamond Ranch Academy and Brigham Young University with sociology degrees, majoring in criminology with a concentration in deviant behavior and juvenile delinquency.

Their homecoming was not as awkward as AJ expected. Trudy got a job at the Martin County jail, and Leigh joined the police academy.

AJ knew his father would have been very proud of each of his family members, working within the community to help families, kids, and teens in trouble. His father had been such a revered judge in this town and made such a difference that the Hudson Scholarship for Troubled Teens and the Hudson Rehabilitation Center was recently named in his honor long after his death. Many local police officers, lawyers, county clerks, and successful business owners spent time in their home at some time or another as foster children or being mentored by AJ's ma and dad. Although AJ and Esther took in eleven foster children over the years, it paled in comparison to the countless children, teens, and families his father had touched within the community. AJ woke up every day trying to be the man his father hoped he would be.

Once the twins moved back home, Esther put them to work with the teenagers in the house on their off-hours when they were not pursuing their careers. She put them in charge of all basement activities, specifically the rehabilitation room since they spent significant time there during their tumultuous childhood.

One evening, shortly after the girls' return home, AJ got home from work, and Esther greeted him at the door.

"AJ, don't get mad, but I have something to tell you."

"Alright," he said, doing his best to stay calm.

"I made you some tea with honey. Eucalyptus tea, like Ma used to make. Let's chat in the kitchen," she suggested.

He followed her nervously into the kitchen and sat down. Holding the warm cup of tea in his hands, he said, "Okay, shoot. What's going on?"

"The chief of police, the new one—Luke's son, Luke Junior—came by this morning. He heard about the room in the basement and the success we've had over the years with some of our more difficult foster kids . . ."

"Esther, how exactly do they know about that room?"

"Leigh, I suspect. She has made quite the impression at the academy."

"Oh no, Esther, what did the chief say exactly? Are we in some kind of trouble? I can get a lawyer here within the hour," he said as his heart palpitated, beginning to panic.

"No, we are not in any trouble. Quite the contrary. The chief said he has a few parents who want to hire us to straighten out their difficult children for a few days or weeks."

"You have got to be kidding me. Esther, I don't know what you have done in that room over the years, and I never asked, but I surely don't want to know about it now."

"AJ, we have fostered many kids over the years, all of whom turned out well. They are respectable people in the community with excellent jobs and thriving families. We did a great job, and now the chief wants us to consider taking in a few wayward teens to help troubled families."

"I don't like the sound of this, and how do we know that this is not a trap by the police? This can't be legal."

"I trust the chief. Actually, it was Leigh's idea. She brought the idea to her sergeant, and he brought it to the chief. The parents will pay us for our efforts."

"Esther, payment for punishment? I don't like this. It has to be criminal."

"It's not punishment, AJ. It's tough love."

"Esther," he said. He took in a deep breath and paused to reflect. Then he placed his hands over hers across the kitchen table. "I have never asked you about your childhood or how *exactly* you discipline all of our kids, but please don't go down this path. No good can come of it. Bringing in other people's children, their parents' consent or not, is not a good idea."

She smiled and said something he had always hoped to hear. "This, AJ, is something the girls and I agreed to do together—a common bond."

Those words would otherwise melt his heart if not for the subject matter.

"We, the three of us, are excited about this," she continued. "Leigh is excited. Trudy wants to help. We, well, we all want to help, along with the police. What could go wrong?"

Chapter Thirty

The Pineapple Fruitcake
Christmas Eve 2020

Dirty Harry and Chet agreed to make the fruitcake this year, against everyone's better judgment. This year of Covid has wreaked havoc on everyone, yet this foolishness continues. Anyway, Gina was adamant that Patty's Christmas wish should continue. So Chet and Harry decide to bake a fruitcake for the new neighbor, Larry.

Early on Christmas Eve, Chet awakens to rain pelting persistently upon the tin roof and coughing from his dad's bedroom.

"Hey, are you feeling alright?" asks Chet, standing by his dad's bed.

"No, I've got a headache. My throat hurts. I won't be going to work today."

"How can I help?"

"Make me some tea with honey. Please bring mc a few Motrin. Pick up a Covid test kit from CVS when you get a chance. I'll call my doctor and see if I can get a telehealth visit later today. Also, just in case it's Covid, wear a mask the next time you come into this room."

"Sure, and what about the fruitcake? We were supposed to make it today."

"That's the least of my worries. Larry is not going to care about a stupid cake."

"Right. Sure. Maybe I'll call Luna. She can help me make it. I don't want the ladies in the neighborhood to be mad about us not baking a cake this year. I don't think they like us very much as it is. Let's not make enemies."

"Do what you like, Chet. Just get me some Motrin and tea, please. Go!"

"Hello?" Luna answers her cell phone with a tentative tone. "Chet, is everything okay? What's up?"

"Um, I think my dad has Covid. Not sure. I will pick up a few Covid tests for us, but I have to make this fruitcake thing today, and I don't know how to do it. My culinary talent lies only with grilled cheese and scrambled eggs. Can you help?"

"Sure. If your test is negative, I'll come over to help. If it's positive, I'll make it myself."

"Thank you. You're a lifesaver."

"What kind of fruitcake are you making?"

"What kind? I don't know. Are there different kinds? Shit, this sucks."

"No worries. I'll find a recipe on the internet. I'll text you one. My aunt made us a pineapple fruitcake one year. It was pretty good. Well, as far as fruitcakes go. Did you know that Jensen Beach was once the pineapple capital of the world? At one time, over one million pineapples would be sold and exported every year."

"Interesting . . . anyway, when can you come over?"

"Take your Covid test, then we'll talk."

At 2:00 p.m., Luna arrives at Chet's. "I'm wearing my mask just in case. You know, you could have Covid but not show symptoms for a few days."

"Yeah, I'm very well aware. It's all anyone talks about these days. I'm tired of all this Covid talk."

"Same."

"How's your dad feeling?" she asks, placing two Publix bags on the kitchen counter.

"He's got Covid, but he's feeling better. Thanks for asking."

"I've got everything we need. You need to Venmo me twenty-four dollars and seventeen cents."

"Of course."

"Did you know a pineapple fruitcake was brought along the Apollo 11 space mission? Well... they didn't eat it and now you can find it at the Smithsonian National Air and Space Museum in Washington, DC.”

“Wow, is that so?” Chet does his best feigning interest with a nod and a slight smile.

“Let’s start. I need a mixing bowl, a can opener, a whisk, and a large spoon.”

“Huh? Well, I know where the can opener is.”

“Ugh, I’ll find everything else,” says Luna, opening and closing cabinets and drawers, looking for the mixing bowl and whisk.

“Sorry, I don’t spend much time in the kitchen.”

“Obvi. Hey—a Rubik’s Cube.” Luna, excited now, grasps the toy from the kitchen window ledge. “Sometimes I can just look at a puzzle, and I can unleash its secrets. Not this one. This is the original three-by-three. Where did you get this?”

“Well, it’s not mine. It’s my dad’s. Here’s something no one else knows.” Chet takes a deep breath, pauses for a moment, then continues. “He came home with this cube after his disappearance.” Luna hands the Rubik’s Cube to Chet.

“What? Really? So weird!”

“Yeah, and that’s not all.”

“What else?”

“Well, there’s a book.”

“A book?”

“Yeah, *The Power of Now*, I think. Not sure. He keeps it under his pillow. Very strange. To be honest, I'm afraid to ask. I think I don't want to know what happened to him. Does that make me a bad person?"

"No. Not at all. I guess it may be painful to hear. I mean, with him losing his pinky finger and all."

"Yeah."

"Yeah, great book, by the way," says Luna enthusiastically. "Read it. Loved it. It was required reading in my philosophy class. My teacher is a big fan of Eckhart Tolle. It teaches you to live in the moment. Enjoy today and find time for reflection and your purpose in life on a larger scale."

"Sounds deep."

"Very. Let's get mixing."

With the cake in the oven, Luna suggests, "Hey, when you're ready, I'll go over to Larry's with you."

"Great, thanks so much." Chet could not have been happier. "You're the best!" he says with a wide smile.

"I know," she giggles, tossing her hair back with her right hand. "No autographs, please."

Chet moves to hug her, but Luna shrieks, "No, I don't like to be touched! Sorry. It's not you. It's me."

"Famous classic breakup line," he says flatly.

"Um, we were never dating . . . so?"

"That's not what I meant. It's just a famous thing people say when they want to break up with someone."

"Oh! I wouldn't know. Anyway, when the timer rings, take the cake out of the oven, wait a few hours for it to cool, then take it out of the pan and lather it with the cream cheese icing. Call me when you want to deliver it."

Luna's phone buzzes, and she glances at the screen. "It's my mom wondering where I am. She thinks I'm at the tennis court."

"Well, that explains your outfit. Why can't you tell your mom you're here?"

"Um, I'm a teenage girl . . . you're a teenage boy that's older than me, so . . ."

"Parents always think the worst! See you later?"

"Yup. Text me."

At 6:00 p.m., Luna gets a text.

> Now a good time? [cake emoji]
>
> [check mark emoji] [Walking lady emoji] now. Perfect timing, actually. Family starts arriving 4 dinner in 30.

"Masks?" Luna asks hesitantly as she approaches Chet on the sidewalk, playing with the mask on her wrist.

"We're outdoors and won't get too close, so no. Probably not necessary."

Luna had noticed Chet taking a photo of the cake. "Pic for your Insta?"

"No. It's just for Snapchat. Proud of our cake—sending it to a few friends. They will be amazed. Do you want to take a pic?"

"No, I don't have any social media profiles to post it to."

"Really? Why?"

"Most girls my age are surgically attached to their phones, but I'm not falling into the social media trap. These phones are a product of surveillance capitalism. Companies use our personal info and life choices to market products to us for profit. I'm not buying into it. No one needs to know that much about me. It's creepy."

"Just the other day"—Chet's eyes widen excitedly—"I was talking about wanting a fishing knife, and the next morning, an ad appeared on my Insta page. So I bought it. I kind of like that my phone knows what I need."

"It's not your phone, dummy. It's people surveilling your life. You know, everything you consume, social media, food, or otherwise, is what you become. Ugh, never mind. Do what you want," says Luna with a shrug and shake of her head.

Chet's mouth opens, but he swallows back his words. He realizes there is no winning an argument with Luna. She's tough. Instead, he arches his left eyebrow and cracks a crooked smile.

"What are you doing with your face? Fix your face, Chet." Luna motions her hand in a circular motion around his face. "That expression makes you look like a weirdo. Don't do that again."

"Noted," Chet says, lowering his eyes to the sidewalk.

When Chet and Luna arrive, Larry is sitting on an Adirondack chair on his porch.

"Merry Christmas," says Chet.

"Thank you. Same to you." Larry returns the sentiment.

"Love your Christmas sweater," says Luna.

"Drunk Santa. It's my favorite." Larry reaches for the fruitcake. "I heard a lot about this fruitcake thing. The fruitcake has quite the reputation around here."

"Yeah, just coincidence. But be careful," suggests Luna. "I hear this fruitcake is to die for."

"Very funny," says Chet, then turns to Luna for a high five.

"Well, I have a strategy. Not gonna die. I'm not eating it right away. Gonna leave it on the island in the kitchen for a few days. I should be safe if I don't eat it over the Christmas holiday."

"Um, technically, my uncle never ate it. He swerved off the road and smashed into a streetlight. It was an accident, though. The fruitcake just happened to be in the passenger seat. So maybe don't take the cake out for a drive."

"Maybe I'll keep it in the garage refrigerator for a few days, where it can't do any harm," Larry smirks, seemingly happy with his solution.

"You guys are being ridiculous. It's not haunted or cursed. It's just a fruitcake. It can't hurt you," says Luna sternly.

"Right," Larry says, pointing a finger in her direction."Still, keeping it in the garage to be safe. Looks delicious, though. Thank you."

"It's a pineapple fruitcake," Luna, excited now, explains to Larry about Jensen Beach and pineapples. She goes on and on.

"Thanks for the history lesson," says Larry, looking overwhelmed. "Most girls your age are usually interested in gossip, clothes, and boys."

"I'm not most girls," Luna quips back. "What would *you* know about girls my age?"

"Okay, Luna, time to go. You've got family coming over." Chet gestures with his thumb toward Luna's house as her aunt is just arriving with a car full of kids.

"Oh, that's the bad aunt," she clarifies. "My good aunt gifted us the house in her will. The bad aunt is still mad about it."

"We gotta go. Have a merry Christmas. Enjoy the cake." Chet adds all the extra goodbye niceties.

Three days later, feeling empowered that he survived the curse of the Laguna Palms fruitcake, Larry brings the fruitcake into the house and cuts himself a slice, then another, and another.

About a half hour later, as he steps out of the shower, the doorbell rings. The FedEx lady drops off a package and returns to her vehicle.

Not realizing the doorbell rang only to warn that a delivery has arrived on the porch, Larry dresses quickly and races down the stairs. Midway down the staircase, feeling dizzy, he trips and falls, breaking his wrist and dislocating his shoulder.

Chapter Thirty-One

Penance
December 12, 2022
Dr. Davis

I sleep poorly. I lay in bed, terrified of what's to come. I'm overcome with an odd feeling that something sinister is about to happen. It's palpable, like a scent in the air, and I have a keen nose for trouble. Scared would not be sufficient enough a word to describe how I feel right now. Terrified would be better.

I stare at the ceiling and accumulate another list in my head. This time, it's a list of regrets.

I regret not going to law school. Law is what I really wanted to study. My parents steered me in a different direction. "You're so good in science but a terrible communicator," Mom would say. Yeah, sure, I'm a terrible communicator. My sister bullied me into submission. I was afraid to speak out.

I regret not staying together with my high school girlfriend, Irene. She was intelligent, beautiful, and kind. My best friend, Joey, convinced me to dump her. "How can you enjoy college with a girlfriend weighing you down?" She married Joey a year later, my supposed best friend. I'm such a sucker sometimes.

I regret not traveling abroad to help kids in need. I will do this as soon as I can get out of here. I desperately need to escape this town.

I stop there. This list only makes me feel even more miserable, if that's even possible. I remember the maze analogy the tall lady suggested I think about. These three regrets and choices I made are the precise adjustments I would make in my life's path. I'm hit all at once with the epiphany that doing one thing differently is the same as doing everything differently. A calm comes over me as I lie in bed and think about everything.

Unexpectedly, the door opens, and my heart races. This time, a short, chunky, toad-looking woman enters. She walks toward me smiling, with a wild look and a face full of moles or maybe they're warts—a perfect character actress for any horror movie. I remind myself once again that I will NEVER watch another horror movie.

"What happened to the tall lady?" My voice cracks.

She does not answer my question. Instead, she stares into my eyes, expressionless, scaring me from the inside out. The look on her face turns my blood to ice. I swallow past the dryness in my throat. I feel my eyes cloud with tears.

She aggressively grabs my chin. She reaches into her pocket. A tool—sharp, metallic—gleams in her hand. She's smiling now, a wide eerie grin . . . maniacal.

She encloses her fingers around a pair of needle-nose pliers and forces open my mouth. My eyes widen in total panic, and I begin to perspire profusely. I'm burning up from the inside out. Her breath smells like rubbish. I want to puke. Instead, I lose control of my bladder. I try to pull away. She's too strong. She yanks out—steals, rather— four molars and plants them proudly in her pocket, one after another, like serial killers collect trophies. Her eyes bore into mine, and she pats her pocket and grins proudly. I'm suddenly yanked back into the reality that my misery *can* worsen.

Before passing out from the excruciating pain, the last words I hear are: "In the end, Dr. Davis,... we all get what we deserve. May this be a constant reminder of the four lives you stole."

Chapter Thirty-Two

Ladies Luncheon, Drift Kitchen & Bar
January 2021
Holly

Inside the Hutchinson Shores Resort lies an exquisite restaurant where you can enjoy fresh sea air, the serenity of the ocean, and culinary expertise. The Drift is one of our favorites. We include this one in the ladies' luncheon rotation often.

A large seaside table for the four of us invites us to a beautiful afternoon. Without a cloud in the sky and a bottle of prosecco waiting for us, there is nothing like the comfort of friends, a tropical setting and great food on this beautiful island we call home.

"Hello, ladies, my name is Buddy. I'll be your waiter this afternoon." Our server greets us with four champagne flutes. "Are we celebrating any special occasions this afternoon?"

"Ladies' afternoon out," Greta declares with an eager smile.

"Shall I retrieve a few strawberries from the kitchen?"

"Indeed," Gina affirms.

We toast and clink our strawberry-garnished champagne flutes.

"To a new year. May it bring good tidings, opportunities, health, happiness, and prosperity," suggests Gina.

"Sing it, sister," says Chloe. "My online classroom over Covid nearly killed me. I'm happy things are mostly back to normal."

"Me too," I agree. "Glad the kids are back in school, but sadly, Bradley is back at work. I have to say, it was nice having him home full-time. It sounds boring, I know, but the kids went back to school in August, and for five months, Bradley and I had the house to ourselves all day, walks along the beach in the evenings once the kiddos trailed off to sleep, and already I miss his cuddles. Our romance could not have been more alive."

"Please don't tell me you're pregnant," quips Gina.

"Not a chance," I say. "I've got enough mess and mischief to last a lifetime."

We laugh, and Chloe adds, "Covid, for me, was a little too much togetherness. I had my classroom babies over Zoom, and Fred was a constant annoyance. He's on a fitness kick, bouncing about the living room, squatting and jumping around, then destroying the kitchen with his putrid protein shakes. Additionally, there's Luna, researching every subject known to the universe on the internet. Well, it's nice to be free."

"I have a brand new respect for Harrington and his dad duties. While working from home, I understood firsthand how much work it is to keep the kids fed, educated, and entertained. He does such a great job with the kids. I think I'll keep him," Greta insists.

Buddy returns with a blue crab cake appetizer. "Compliments of the chef," he offers.

"Say hello for me." Gina winks at the waiter.

"Another fan?" I ask.

"Maybe," Gina says, looking toward the kitchen, hoping to steal a glimpse of him. "Let's just say I know him well, but we never actually met."

"Really?" asks Chloe. "I hear he's newly divorced. Maybe he'll come out to greet us later."

"Hope so." Gina's cheeks turn pink.

When Buddy returns, we all order the Drift Salad, a signature item on the lunch menu. The salad comes with field greens, heirloom tomatoes, English cucumber, pickled onions, roasted beets, goat cheese, and a citrus vinaigrette. We accompany the salad with two shrimp tacos orders to share.

Midway through our meal, my phone rings. "Shit, it's the school," I say quietly.

"Oh no," "Crap," and "Hope everything is okay," say the girls.

I answer and I'm not able to say much. Can't get a word in edgewise. The principal goes on and on about all three of my children. I nervously tap my foot under the table. I say, "Uh-huh," and "Alright, okay," and "Yes, we can meet in the morning."

"What's going on?" begs Gina. Everyone stops eating. "Spill it!"

"Well," I say, then let out a laugh I had to expel.

"What's so funny!" demands Greta.

"Rosco peed on a kid during recess."

The ladies gasp, but I continue, "Some shitty bully kid at school was making fun of Emmett, saying he runs like a girl. So Rosco pulled out his penis and pissed on this kid's leg. Oh, and that's not all. Rosie then tells all the kids in the playground that the bully—they wouldn't tell me his name, by the way—has tea parties with teddy bears and that he has the nerve to talk about Emmett running like a girl when he cuddles with stuffed animals and dolls. Rosie then pushes the kid. And, well . . . the Kelly kids landed themselves in the principal's office."

"I *love* those little fuckers," says Gina.

"Me too," says Greta and Chloe in unison.

"Raising kids is not for the faint of heart," I lament.

"You got that right," says Greta.

"Look, if I can keep these kids out of the hospital, the newspapers, and jail, I feel as though I've concluded my God-given duty."

"Funny," Chloe laughs. Let's start with helping them get through elementary school, shall we?"

A few moments later, Chef strolls over to the table. He snatches Gina's hand for a delicate kiss.

"So very nice to finally meet you," he says, pulling out a chocolate heart wrapped in red foil and placing it in her hand.

"Thank you," says Gina, cheeks flushed.

He leaves her with his business card and offers, "Please call me. You won't be disappointed."

Oohs and aahs from the rest of us only leave Gina more embarrassed. I never knew she was capable of this particular emotion, and my heart melts a little along with hers.

"A real *suavecito*," I say. When the ladies look confused, I explain, "It's another Latina expression. You know, a smooth talker. The chatter around town is that he's a bit of a womanizer. So be careful."

As Chef returns to the kitchen, the hostess hands him a package. He grabs it with his left hand. His hand, shockingly, is missing his ring finger.

The four of us keep each other's gaze in a dreadful stare until Chef returns to the kitchen.

"He hated his ex-wife so much he removed his whole finger along with the wedding ring?" I offer, trying to be funny.

"Another person with a missing digit," says Greta. "Coincidence?"

While we're all looking at each other, wide-eyed, Chloe raises our third prosecco bottle and asks our waiter, "Can we have the cork for the prosecco? We've got to go. Three bottles are too much. We need to drink with moderation, ladies."

"Who is this moderation we are supposed to be drinking with?" Gina snatches the bottle away from Chloe and pours the remainder into our glasses. "Corks are for quitters. Drink up, ladies."

Chapter Thirty-Three

Super Bowl Party
February 7, 2021
Larry

L arry tells no one of his fall down the stairs. Instead, for the next six weeks, he quietly recovers at home. He hides the cast on his wrist by draping his suit jacket over his arm when the neighbors are in sight. It was a clumsy fall, for which he didn't want to muster any attention his way with conspiracy theories or ghost stories about the fruitcake. It was just an accident, he reminds himself—an awkward fall.

Today, the neighbors will gather around the cul-de-sac for the Super Bowl. Hosting too many people indoors is still frowned upon due to recent Covid recommendations. Larry watches Fred from his porch. He erects a twenty-foot inflatable screen, projector, speaker system, and cable box to prepare for the big game later this evening when the Tampa Bay Buccaneers will ante up against the Kansas City Chiefs.

At 6:30 p.m., during kickoff, Larry peers out the window. The neighborhood kids are racing around on their scooters, bikes, and one little girl is on roller skates. The guys are transfixed on the screen to see who wins the coin toss. Nearly everyone is wearing a Brady jersey. Some wear Tampa Bay Brady jerseys, while others wear New England Brady jerseys. Just one holdout—Harry—is wearing a Chiefs jersey. That's the Harry the community loves, always rooting for the underdog.

By halftime, as The Weeknd is performing, Larry feels he has to join in the fun. All of this activity is painful for him to watch from the window. Never before did he truly understand the term FOMO. The fear of missing out is tearing him apart. He grabs a jacket from the hall tree, drapes it over his broken wrist, and races outside to enjoy the fun.

"Hey, Larry," squeals Harry. "Where the hell have you been lately? I haven't seen you for weeks."

"I've been working. I'm swamped with proposals for clients. My office laid off a few real estate agents and office staff. It's on the rest of us to step up," he lies, running his fingers through his red hair with his good hand.

"Big shake-ups in the real estate market?" asks Harry.

"Yes, sir. The real estate market is booming as we climb out of the pandemic. Lots more retirees looking to move to Florida."

Harry hands him a Budweiser that he hasn't yet opened.

"Budweiser? You got anything else?"

"It's the Super Bowl, bro. Gotta celebrate with American sponsors for America's favorite pastime."

"Alright then, Bud, it is." Larry instinctively grabs for the beer with his broken hand exposing his cast.

"What happened to your hand?" asks Harry, making a whacking-off gesture with his right hand. "Too much personal attention during lockdown?"

"Yeah, that's it. You got me!"

"No, really, what happened?"

"I fell down the stairs a few weeks back and injured my wrist."

"When?"

This was the question he dreaded.

"Two weeks ago." Another lie.

As Harry trails off to grab another beer, Chloe, Gina, and Greta approach Larry.

Chloe asks, "How are you? We're all worried. We haven't seen you lately."

"We thought maybe the fruitcake killed you," Greta says jokingly with a forced smile.

"No, the cake was delicious." Larry smiles nervously, darting his eyes back and forth between

Chloe and Greta. "Please tell Luna and Chet I enjoyed it."

"How's your wrist? I just heard you broke it," asks Gina.

"I'll be fine. I fell down the stairs a few weeks ago."

In unison, all three ladies mutter, "Oh."

He can feel the weight of the judgmental stares. These women are so nosy, he thinks. He wishes they would leave him alone.

"Thanks for coming out," says Chloe. "Luna and I made a Mexican dip. You've got to try it. It's fantastic."

"Will do." Larry nods and walks over toward the other guys to join in on their conversation about fishing the flats in the Florida Keys for bonefish, tarpon, permit, and barracuda.

"Last month, we caught redfish and spotted sea trout in Key Largo," says Fred.

"I'm gonna head down to Big Pine Key next weekend with Chet to catch some tarpon if any of you'd like to come with me," offers Harry.

By the end of the game, the men are drunk, and the ladies swoon over a sweaty Brady—a perfect end to an ideal match.

After a vigorous clean-up, Harry approaches Larry as he heads home.

"Hey, bro, thanks for coming out. Let's get together again soon. Sorry about what happened to your wrist."

"Yeah, thanks."

Unexpectedly, Harry grabs Larry and brings him in for a big hug. Upon arriving home, Larry feels something in his back pocket. He pulls out a crumpled note that reads:

Don't trust anyone.

Chapter Thirty-Four

The Key
December 16, 2022
Dr. Davis

I wake up groggy, my lips sticking to my teeth. I need water. I feel numb. As I sit up in the bed, I feel the tug of an IV hooked up through my hand. I wonder just how long I've been asleep, drugged. I feel a dull pain on both sides of my lower jaw, and I'm brought back to my last memory. I must have been asleep for quite some time because the pain I initially felt has subsided substantially.

My eyes dart over to the marks I made on the wall to mark the many days of my stay here in hell. Those twelve marks are useless; I'm sure this is not the thirteenth day. The US military will tell you it takes approximately fifteen days to break a man's spirit. Mine was lost long ago. I feel hopeless, like a cancer patient, cells destroying the body from within, killing me slowly, painfully. I stop myself—no time for a pity party. Somehow, I pull myself together.

The diaper I'm wearing is full. I rip it off in disgust. Tears stream down my face. I'm angry, sad, humiliated, but also defiant in my determination to get out of here. I've got to put my critical thinking skills to work.

"Think, think," I mutter out loud. There has to be a fail-safe in this room somewhere. What if one of my captors got trapped in here by accident somehow? There has to be a hidden key somewhere in this room. I've got to look around and hope that if there's a spare key, it's within my arm's reach of these shackles.

Everyone knows that the best place to hide anything is in plain sight. I use my eyes and trace my gaze along every inch of the gray-painted concrete wall. Not much to find. There's the window and the metal plate I hit for the hologram, and nothing else stands out. Maybe by the door, there's a spare key above the frame. Sadly, if the key is hiding there, I can't reach it. My reach is limited, and I feel defeated.

I change direction. I've got to get them to unlock my shackles. They promised I would be released soon. The tall lady promised me. Now I'm wondering if I will ever get out of here alive.

Static from the speaker above . . . then, a voice. It's the tall lady. I could recognize her sweet, soft voice anywhere.

"Dr. Davis, the worst part of your confinement has concluded. Please know that we are all on your side. We are rooting for your recovery. You will be released soon. I promise. I will visit you in the morning to discuss the terms of your release. In the meantime, rest. Dream big dreams about the second chance you have been given and new ways in which you will choose to live your life for the betterment of society instead of your lust, greed, and vanity."

When she's done speaking, I trace my hand around the bed frame, the mattress, the pillow—nothing. I creep gingerly off the bed onto the floor. I feel for anything unusual under the bed—still nothing. I sit, looking around the room, thinking about what place, if any, someone could hide a key. Where would *I* hide it if I were trapped within the confines of this space? Frustrated, I stand on my bed to get a better visual, a larger perspective of the room.

And just like that, the fluorescent lights flicker as if cued by my demand, and something shiny is illuminated on the windowsill. The sill is too high. I can't reach it. I roll the IV pole along with me as far as my shackles can take me. I reach the window, using the pole to knock the key off its resting spot. It falls to the floor, dust cascading through the air, and lands by my feet.

"Freedom," I whisper to myself, "sweet freedom." My curious tongue finds the four holes in my mouth where my teeth used to be—a constant reminder of what *I* have done and what *they* have done to me. My heart pounds and a smile forces its way onto my face. "Time to make a plan," I say out loud, but those words echo endlessly, bouncing across the basement walls in the confines of this hellscape.

Chapter Thirty-Five

Sailfish Splash Waterpark
July 2021
Holly

The water park saved my sanity over the pandemic. It was one of the places that only closed for a few short weeks during Covid. It was the perfect way to spend a few hours away from the house and homeschooling. Since then, we've habitually visited the water park at least a few times a month. I love a relaxing afternoon lying in the sun, catching up on a good book while the kids can splash around safely with lifeguards to watch over them at all times. We have a private beach past the dunes in our neighborhood, but the kids tend to run off and are difficult to wrangle back, so the water park suits us well.

As soon as we arrive at the water park, Emmett starts barraging me with endless questions. I've never met a kid more inquisitive.

"Mommy, why is the water wet? Why can't I pee in the pool?" Then, the final question: "Are you going to have more babies?"

"No, honey, no more babies. You three are all I need," I say assuringly.

"Did the doctor sew up your butt?"

"Babies don't come from your butt, silly. They come from your tummy. Boys are so stupid," says Rosie.

I'm trying really hard not to laugh.

"Your tummy?" Emmett looks bewildered. "How do they get out?"

Then Rosie asserts with authority, "Your belly button, dummy."

I let out a faint giggle.

Emmett lifts his shirt and looks at his belly button. "Mommy, I don't want to have babies."

I nearly choked on the water I just sipped. I guess it's time for Bradley and I to chat soon about those pesky birds and bees.

"Where's Rosco?" I say, trying to change the subject.

"He's wrapped up in beach towels," says Rosie.

"I'm a burrito. Burritos don't swim," claims Rosco from behind a beach chair.

I walk behind the chair and find him wrapped tightly in beach towels, lying flat on the concrete. "Well, they do today. But not after I take a few bites. Yum, yum." I pretend to eat him. "Let's go. I'll go down the slide with you," I promise.

"Hooray!" all three cheer.

I feel like a rock star when they get excited for me to play with them. Something so small feels so good sometimes. It's the little things that bring the most joy in life, I remind myself.

By the time we return from the slide to our beach chairs, Greta has arrived with Ana and Eva.

"Hey, you," I say.

"Sorry, we're late. Harrington and Fred are working on some new invention at my house. We barely escaped unharmed."

The kids run off to the splash playground while we continue our conversation.

"Be careful," I yell out.

"Take turns under the dump bucket and the slides. No pushing," demands Greta, but I don't think they're listening.

"What idea are they scheming about these days? I wish they could talk to the Apple people and get them to invent a screen you can read in daylight. You know, like the Kindle Paperwhite." I hold up my phone, squinting. "I can't see shit on my phone at this time of day!"

"Right? I totally agree. They're working on a motion detector to hang in the trees in the front yard, with a camera for surveillance."

"Didn't the Ring doorbell people invent something like that already?"

"Not like this one. This is designed with a 360-degree camera covertly hidden within a two-story birdhouse."

"What?"

"Yeah, it's pretty swanky. Inconspicuous."

"What are they trying to capture?" I ask. Now I *have* to know!

"They hope to capture whatever the hell seems to be going on at the Hudson house. Fred said Chloe wouldn't be happy about the spying, but he's convinced something shady is happening over there."

"How so?"

"Not sure. The only time I see them is on trash day. Then there are the black SUVs that come and go at odd hours. That's all I can tell you, or I'll have to kill you."

"Very funny. But keep me in the loop. I love a juicy story," I admit.

We intend to stay until closing. Wearing these kids out before bed is a high priority for me. Bradley comes home tonight, and I want to find some quiet time just for the two of us. I can't wait to tell him all about how our kids envision childbirth.

But by 3:00 p.m., storm clouds roll in, and we've got to get packed up quickly. There are three great truths about Florida summers. The first is that weather apps are unreliable. Second, you will sweat in crevices you didn't know you had. And third, late afternoon thunderstorms are a summer staple, often more powerful than a hurricane. Plan your days accordingly.

I pack my kids' towels, water bottles, and snacks into my beach bag. The sky begins to cry. Tiny raindrops, then larger ones, pelt against our faces. When Greta hastily grabs for her beach bag, a Rubik's Cube falls out.

Chapter Thirty-Six

The Lady in the Park
August 2021
Holly

I can't sleep. My mind races about the kids starting school next week. First grade is a big deal; preparing the kids mentally and providing all the necessary school supplies is more of a task than I imagined.

I get up, get dressed, and walk through the dog park to settle nervous energy and anxious thoughts.

The streetlights illuminate along the path. Crickets, cicadas, and frogs sing—a beautiful nocturnal chorus. Males produce the loudest sounds, trying to attract female attention.

The park is empty, which is not surprising for 4:30 a.m. I make a few loops around the park path before settling on a bench to enjoy the insect harmonies.

Fifteen minutes pass, and my nerves start to settle. I create a list in the notes section of my phone about all the many school supplies to pick up at Target to prepare the kids for school next week. I create another list of apparel I need to buy: backpacks, sneakers, colored button-down shirts, et cetera. Instead of feeling overwhelmed, I'm beginning to feel better prepared. Ready to tackle the challenge of preparing triplets for first grade.

At 5:00 a.m., Willa arrives with her two little mutts on leash. She waves as she approaches, then sits beside me. She's wearing baggy joggers and a red button-down sweater that reeks of mothballs. I try my best not to wince too obviously. I lower my head and turn away. I move myself further down the bench, giving her more space. A nice gesture for her comfort? Nope. I had to escape the wretched scent emanating from her sweater. I'm not sure what it is about old folks and mothballs. Maybe it's just a Florida thing.

"Good morning. You're up early. I never see you out here so early in the morning. Is everything alright?"

"Yeah, just a short walk and a head start to seize the day," I explain.

"So . . . trouble sleeping?"

"Yeah, you got me. The kids start first grade next week. My mind is overstimulated with an extensive to-do list. Sleep comes sparingly these days."

"Isn't there an app for that?"

"There are quite a few apps to get your mind at ease and ready to sleep," I offer. "Some apps play calming noises or music, while others read you bedtime stories."

"I'm not surprised. Your generation allows your phones to rule over your whole lives."

"You're not wrong, Willa," I admit. "The last time I saw you was at the House of Refuge. Did you discover any interesting treasure?" I ask, changing the subject away from my problems.

"Well, as a matter of fact, I did. I found an old coin dating back to when the Spaniards arrived three hundred years ago. Maybe washed ashore after a storm from a shipwreck."

"Wow, I guess they call this the Treasure Coast for a reason."

"The shore rewards us with treasure from the past whenever a storm passes. The great balance of nature's fury and nature's beauty."

"That's quite profound, Willa," I say, impressed by her perspective.

"The universe can only survive with the right balance," she continues. "For every good or positive experience, there's a villain and trauma. It's the human experience."

"Hmm," I say. There's so much she just packed into that one sentence. I open the notes app on my phone and type in word for word what she just said. I need to ponder that thought later in greater detail. I feel inspired. It could be a lyric for a future song.

While I'm typing the note into my phone, Willa claims, "You're a catalyst for change around here, you know?"

"What? I'm sorry, me? What do you mean by that?"

Willa opens her backpack and pulls out tarot cards wrapped in a beautiful Italian silk scarf. She shuffles the deck and then asks me to pick a card.

"What's this all about?" I ask, bewildered.

"You'll see."

I pull out a card from the middle of the deck. It depicts a man in a cloak holding a lantern in his right hand and a long staff in his left. The number nine in Roman numerals, IX, is at the top of the card. The words, The Hermit, are at the bottom.

"The seeker," she says.

"The seeker?"

"Yes, you are the truth seeker. The hermit holds the lantern to uncover the path before him. He steps forward to see where to go next. He knows everything will not be revealed at once. In his left hand, the staff reveals his subconscious mind. The staff, a sign of power and authority, will seek justice for what the path unveils in due time."

"I don't understand what that means," I say.

"You have been brought here to uncover a truth, an atrocity, and bring something sinister to light, like the hermit illuminating the path. You will shine a light on a great injustice. You will bring balance back to the community."

Willa takes the card from my hand and places it back in the deck. She wraps the deck in the scarf and puts it in her backpack. She stares directly into my eyes. My stomach feels queasy as she slowly and purposefully utters these words: "This is your destiny, Holly. You can't outrun destiny!"

She stands and briskly walks away with her dogs without uttering another word.

My hands tremble. I rub them on my leggings. I watch her walk away. Within seconds, she disappears into the darkness.

The red maple trees rustle in the wind, demanding my attention. I look away. A squirrel in the trees deadlocks its big brown eyes on mine, tail wagging in alarm—warning me. It understands that I'm scared, spooked. If a caption had been written above its head, it would have read RUN!

Upon returning home, as I make my way up the stairs, I hear a whistle and turn abruptly. Willa is standing on the sidewalk without her dogs, arms stoically by her sides, eyes staring, expressionless, looking straight through me. I rush inside and lock the door. I may never sleep again.

Chapter Thirty-Seven

Hope
December 17, 2022
Dr. Davis

Lust, greed, and vanity? I can't stop thinking about what the tall lady said yesterday. I'm well aware of the seven deadly sins. Have they forgotten about wrath? How will they know I won't seek revenge when I'm released? Now I'm skeptical I will ever be released. Held against my will in the basement of the Hudson house, how do they know that I won't contact the police once they let me go? Maybe the police are involved? My mind runs wild with conspiracy theories.

I feel panic kick in, so I pull myself out of this dark spiral. The places your mind goes when left to your own devices, alone in the darkness, save a few noisy, barely working lights above, are terrifying.

Often, I catch myself hallucinating. Monsters lurk in the shadows. Ghosts of my childhood torment me. A shadowy figure appears sporadically in the dead of night in the darkest recess of this prison cell. Logically, I'm aware that I must be hallucinating. My medical training has taught me that this type of solitary confinement often manifests with hallucinations, but my logical mind has often been taken over with fear and hopelessness.

The black mass in the corner can't speak, but I swear I can hear my sister's voice. She calls me a wuss, a nerdy weasel. I can smell my sister's perfume, Sweet Honesty, by Avon. This wretched scent brings me back to the evenings I spent alone, locked in my parent's dimly lit closet. Her scent lingers there. I'm angry, humiliated. Why didn't I fight back? Why didn't I tell my mom? I'm ashamed. I find myself cursing at the imaginary shadow of my sister lurking in the corner, trying to break me.

"I hate you!" I yell aloud in the emptiness of this room, the emptiness of my soul. I won't let her break me. I promise myself I will get out of here. I've got the key to escape. But how can I unlock these shackles?

The loneliness is excruciating, the silence deafening. Simon & Garfunkel's song, *The Sound of Silence*, repeats in my head over and over. The lyrics torture me. I create my own new lyrics. Hello darkness you're *not* my old friend. I'll *never* talk with you again. I will NEVER again listen to this song if I get out of here alive.

I long for the sights, sounds, and scents of the hospital. The sirens, constant chatter at the nurse's station, squeaky gurneys, and antiseptic smell are welcoming thoughts. I also miss the hum of my refrigerator, the chime of my grandfather clock, and the thudding clang of the air conditioner kicking on and off at home. My home seems a million miles away, but only one mere mile lies between us.

Today, the tall lady returns and sits beside me on my bed. I knew she was on her way before she opened the door and entered the room. In the darkness and the silence, my senses heighten, and I can smell her coconut-scented lotion and strawberry shampoo. I feel her presence before she even enters the room.

She sits beside me, our legs touch, and I'm immediately aroused, just like the last time she touched me—a side effect of solitude. The touch sensation is heightened. When I turn toward her, I get lost in her eyes. Many people have blue eyes with yellow tones or brown specks, but hers . . . they sparkle like sapphires.

"Dr. Davis, I am here to tell you my story." She lowers her eyes to her lap, where her hands fold one over the other. She is perfectly still. "My story begins two years ago. I was a new mom. My husband left me weeks later. Suddenly, I was battling the pain of a failed marriage and postpartum depression. This is not an excuse, but one day after running errands, exhausted from little sleep, upon returning home, I fell into my bed to nap, forgetting all about my son in the car's back seat. A neighbor passing by heard him crying. He broke the car window, removed my child, then called the police. The county removed my son from my care, and he now lives with my ex-husband."

"I am so sorry," I say, but these words feel unworthy to help heal the pain she suffered. There are no healing words for this moment.

She takes a deep breath, continuing to look down at her hands and continues with her story. "I have since learned that over one thousand children have died in the back seats of cars since 1990. I fully understand the magnitude of my actions. I'm telling you this story because I could be angry with my husband for leaving me, spiraling into depression and exhaustion. I could be angry with my neighbor. All he had to do was ring my doorbell. I would have answered and unlocked the car. I could be angry he called the police, which led to losing my child to my ex-husband. I could be angry at my doctor for prescribing the drugs that made me sleepy. There's lots to be angry about. At first, I *was* angry, then sad, then suicidal."

She gently reaches for my hand, squeezing it tightly. "I was brought here in the cover of night last year. I spent a few weeks in this very bed contemplating what I've done and ways to make positive changes to my life. So, upon my release, I attended nursing school. When I received my degree, I decided to work with tiny babies in the neonatal unit. I now help premature babies survive and thrive."

She must feel proud of her accomplishments because a slight smile begins to emerge. "I am working my way back to being able to see my son again. But I must say that I have enjoyed the journey back in retrospect. There's a lot that I have learned about myself and the joy of helping others in their time of need."

I feel as though I should say something, but her story leaves me with a loss for words.

"Your journey here has been part of my journey. Number five on the list is 'Pay it forward.' You are *my* pay-it-forward. I sincerely hope that when you're released, you look me up. I would enjoy sharing a cup of coffee or a cocktail."

She hands me a folded note with her phone number. I memorize it for fear it may be taken away.

"Thank you," I say sincerely.

She takes a remote out of her pocket and presses a green button on the top. A door opens, and a bathroom is revealed. How did I miss that? But now that the door is open, I can clearly see the grooves etched in the concrete. She removes my shackles.

"Please shower, shave, and trim your hair. You will soon be prompted to sign the nondisclosure agreement tied to the deed for your home. Please keep your time here secret. If you need to talk about it, look me up. I'll be here for you. If you talk about this, they take your home. Don't talk."

I nod my head; I understand. "Thank you," I say. "For everything."

"I'll see you on the other side." She smiles, my heart melts, and tears of joy spill as she walks away.

"Hold up," I shout. "What's your name?"

"You can call me Hope," she says with a genuine heartwarming smile.

"Hope," I mutter aloud, just to hear the word amplified. I remind myself that hope is exactly what I asked for. On day six of my captivity, I tell myself that *God always arrives on time*. I just needed hope. Hope is all I could hold on to. She is exactly what I asked for—my wish. I asked for Hope. God heard me. He granted my wish. I feel renewed and rejuvenated for the first time in forever—dare I say happy?—and I anxiously await the time when I can see her again.

Chapter Thirty-Eight

Esther's Death
April 2018
Judge Hudson

The next three years were some of the happiest in AJ's life. Esther and the girls got along very well. He would often hear them chatting and laughing in the kitchen over tea and snacks until the wee morning hours, even though the girls both had very early wake-up calls.

At this time, all of their fostered children had been placed in forever homes or ushered off to college. From time to time, black SUVs would arrive with a teenager or two, who would be escorted to the basement. From what AJ was told, most temporary occupants were drug addicts. The county would send a nurse to check doses for weening off more potent drugs. AJ tried not to ask too many questions. He feared the answers may be too disturbing.

In the spring of 2018, Esther received terrible news about the stomach pains she had been suffering from recently. It turned out to be stage four pancreatic cancer. One week later, the evening before her second consultation with the oncologist, she died in her sleep. Her last words to their daughters: "Continue the mission."

Chapter Thirty-Nine

The Chocolate Fruitcake
Christmas Eve 2021

Larry doesn't bake. Larry doesn't cook anything at all. His kitchen looks exactly the same as the day he moved in. The dish rack holds one fork, one small white plate, one knife, and a water glass. There is no chance Larry will bake a cake for the exchange this year. He hasn't even thought about it until Gina stops him, walking to his car the morning of Christmas Eve.

"Hey, Larry." Gina waves his way as he walks toward his Ferrari.

"Merry Christmas Eve," he says, walking faster now.

"Hey, who are you gifting the fruitcake to this year?"

"Um, I haven't really thought about it. Forgot about it, actually," he says, opening the car door.

"You have to bake, or at least buy, a fruitcake somewhere and gift it. You can't let the tradition die."

"Die! Exactly that . . . die. That's why maybe I won't participate," he says, walking over to Gina. "Two people are dead due to this stupid fruitcake tradition thing."

"Well, you turned out alright," she asserts, placing her cane-free hand on her hip for added effect.

Now at a loss for words, as he is unwilling to explain his clash with the stairs after eating the cake last year, he offers, "Okay, alright, I'll pick one up on the way home from work tonight. How about I gift it to you? Are you ready to accept the fortune the fruitcake may bestow?" Larry smirks weirdly, maniacal.

"Um, sure. Why not?" Gina says, her voice cracking.

Later that afternoon, Larry places a cake on her doorstep. The cake is nicely decorated with chocolate icing and sprinkles inside of a white box from Publix. Gina wonders if it is actually a fruitcake. It sure doesn't look like one. She thinks Larry probably snatched the first cake he could get a hold of in the cake cooler. Gina lifts the cake and reads the note attached.

Merry Christmas, and may this cake bring you Good Luck!
—Larry

Gina, cake in hand, looks around the neighborhood in both directions. "Oh good, no one is around," she says to herself. She slowly walks over to Holly's house, the only house on the block without a Ring doorbell that could capture her arrival and departure. Gina places the cake and note by the front door, then returns home.

At 4:00 p.m., Holly's cell phone rings.

"Hey, Gina," she says.

"Hey, girl, I noticed you have a package in front of your door."

Opening the door, Holly looks down upon the welcome mat and says, "Oh shit. Oh no, no, no. I don't want this. Fucking Larry!"

"I'm sorry," says Gina.

Holly, holding the cake in her hands, notices the UPS truck. The UPS driver arrives at her house with a few Amazon packages—last-minute gifts for her little ones.

Rosie yells from the kitchen in a singsongy voice, "Mom, Emmett's drinking milk from his shoe."

"Gina, I gotta go," Holly says, abruptly ending the phone call.

"Hi," Holly says as a genius idea infiltrates her brain while the UPS driver approaches the door. Nervously, she breathes in for three seconds, holds for two, and then breathes out for four, as her mindfulness app suggests.

"Merry Christmas."

250

She places Larry's note in the side pocket of her Athleta leggings and hands the UPS driver the cake.

"This is for you," she offers with a smile. "My kids are allergic to chocolate," she lies. "I hope you can enjoy this."

"Oh, thank you very much," the driver says apprehensively. "Funny though, my kids are also allergic to chocolate." She returns the lie. Her right eye twitches when she says that, and now she's blinking more than she should. She pauses, lets out a small sigh, then finally relents. "But . . . I can bring this to my church tonight. After mass, we have a short celebration with the congregation."

"Great idea!" Holly affirms. "Enjoy."

Within seconds of the UPS lady's departure, Holly spots one of the Hudson sisters standing motionless on the sidewalk across from her house. Her lingering stare in Holly's direction gives her the creeps. Her presence makes her feel a bit uneasy. She sure is peculiar. Holly forces a smile and waves.

Suddenly distracted, Holly feels a tug on the back of her shirt and finds Rosie standing behind her. She stares at Holly with a disappointed scowl.

"Mommy, you lied to the mail lady. It's not nice to lie."

"Oh, hush," Holly says. She can't continue this conversation because her phone lights up—Gina's calling.

"Did you just give the fruitcake away to Susan?"

"Um, first, I'm not sure it even is a fruitcake. And second, how well do you know the UPS driver?"

"Well, she's been our UPS driver for three years. I know her pretty well. She has two kids away at college, and one just got married."

Holly wants to ask, Are any of them allergic to chocolate? None of that matters now, she supposes. Instead, she says, "Well, I hope good tidings are bestowed upon her."

"You and me both," says Gina. "You and me both."

At precisely 3:00 a.m., the church's kitchen goes up in flames. The three-alarm fire gets put out within minutes of the arrival of the good men and women of Firehouse 14. There is some damage to the exterior kitchen but no damage to the church's interior. The cause of the fire was later diagnosed as faulty electrical wiring connected to the refrigerator.

There is never any mention of the fire on the local news.

Chapter Forty

The Release
December 17, 2022
Dr. Davis

Once Hope leaves, I enter the bathroom. The room is brightly lit and tastefully decorated. Blue paisley wallpaper, light-blue bathroom rugs, and matching accessories are delicate and warm.

Upon entering, I become hyperaware of my personal hygiene. Disgusting. I shower. Familiar aromas of coconut soap and strawberry shampoo hit my nasal passages. Everything in this bathroom smells like Hope—my heart races. I'm instantly hit with despair. Dark thoughts: Was Hope ever really released? Why, if she was released, would she purchase these items outside of this Godforsaken place? Wouldn't these smells bring her back to this terrible time in her life? Then the realization hits me. Is the pain of this experience part of her joy? Some people say there is a fragile line between pleasure and pain. Maybe she forces herself to relive her time here as a personal punishment—unworthiness. I force myself to believe this rather than my former thought that she was never released. In either scenario, I must save her from her pain. She's become my sole reason for living—a new start.

I let the warm water wash away my misery. As the dirt and grime glide and slither off my skin, so do the sins of the past. I feel clean, restored, pure, in a sense.

Once shaven and hair trimmed, I look in the mirror and hardly recognize myself. I've lost quite a bit of weight, my cheeks hollow, my expression sullen.

I dress myself in the clothes I came here wearing. The shorts and T-shirt hang loose on my much-thinner physique. The clothes feel like an adversary, an artifact of my former self, taunting me . . . a reminder of the man I was, in contrast to the man I have and will become.

My body feels hot and itchy in these clothes. I start to feel anxious. I have the chance to escape. Should I take it? Can I trust Hope? Will I be released soon?

I sit on the bed and wait.

"Hello? Can anyone hear me? I'm dressed and ready to go."

A few minutes pass, then many more. I'm tempted to use the key I found to open the door and leave on my own. But I'm a coward. I won't fight. I lack the temerity necessary to escape on my own. I blame my sister. I used to be brave. No, that's just not true. I was never brave. My sister made sure of that.

One thing I have learned from being held captive for so long is the self-awareness of my strengths and weaknesses, along with the pros and cons of the choices I have made in my life. I remind myself that even inaction is a choice. I lie back on the bed and wait. Waiting for something to happen, that's what cowards do.

After a few hours, the ugly, toad-looking woman appears in the doorframe.

"Oh no, please, no more torture. I was told I'd be released today."

"Yes, you will. I am here to have you sign the release forms. Please read them thoroughly. I will return within thirty minutes."

She drops the paperwork on the floor by the door and then aggressively slams the door shut. The loud clamoring echoes throughout the basement. She must be angry I'm leaving—one less person to torture.

I approach the door, still reluctant to open it with my key. I pick up the seven-page document and read it while standing under the window, daylight illuminating the pages. The nondisclosure agreement keeps me from talking to anyone about my time here. If I tell anyone of my experience here, Hudson Real Estate LLC is awarded ownership of my property in Laguna Palms. I also have to agree to return as part of my community service to help another captive through their experience.

I sign the paperwork and place it back on the floor because I don't want to hand this directly to the toad lady. I don't ever want to get that close to her again.

I yell out to the speaker system that I still cannot find, "I signed the paperwork. Let me out."

A few moments later, I'm blindfolded, walked down a hallway, up eight stairs, out the back door, down seven more stairs, and pushed into a large car that smells like vanilla. I'm forced out of the car about ten minutes later.

"Keep the blindfold on until you can no longer hear the car," a harsh female voice demands. "Remember the rules of the agreement, and enjoy your new life. Not everyone gets a second chance. You are one of the lucky ones. Goodbye, Dr. Davis. We will be in touch regarding your community service requirements soon."

I wait for the car to speed off, then wait an extra few minutes just to be safe. I remove my blindfold and have never been so happy to be home. Gazing at my home, I feel grateful for the life I made for myself. I remind myself to better enjoy everything I took for granted for so long. I lower my eyes to the sidewalk. Gum stains. Do people even chew gum anymore? So many cracks in the sidewalk. The sidewalks should be impeccable with the money it costs to live here. Random thoughts become heightened when you spend so much time alone inside your head, secluded from the outside world.

Reining in my nonsense notions, I race into the house, past the water fountain that desperately needs cleaning. I unlock the door with my key code. Once safely inside, I lock the door and remove the key to my basement prison from my pocket. I hold it tightly in my hand. I fall onto the couch, holding the prison key, and weep like I never have before.

Chapter Forty-One

A Year in Review
2022
Holly

A lot has happened over the past year in the neighborhood. In my personal life, my seven-year-olds are doing well in school and have joined an eight-and-under coach-pitch baseball league, and we're lucky enough that the kids get to play on the same team. Rosie complains about how crude the boys can be. She often complains about booger-picking, farting, smelly armpits, and one boy who likes to grab his balls and smell his hands. However, she enjoys being the team's star hitter with the highest batting average in the league.

The annual Super Bowl party never came to fruition because the guys scored tickets to the Super Bowl. While the boys were off to California, the ladies and I ventured off to Epcot. My advice for attending any Disney park is to travel Super Bowl weekend to escape the crowds. I brought along Francesca to help out with the kiddos. I get vertigo on rides, but the kids enjoy them. While the kids were entertained with any ride they were tall enough to enjoy, the ladies and I hurried off to drink around the world in Epcot's World Showcase. But honestly, we kept coming back to Mexico because their frozen margaritas were delicious.

Larry moved out by the spring, and now Patty's house sits empty. The day before he moved away, However, Fred mentioned to Chloe that one of the Hudson sisters, the ugly one, was caught on his surveillance camera coming to and from Larry's house last Christmas Eve. Fred has some fascinating footage of certain comings and goings at the Hudson house over the past few years. Some of his footage comes from the Ring doorbell, other footage from a camera in his car, and recent footage from his 360-degree birdhouse camera.

By the fall, Fred had become obsessed with surveilling the Hudson house. He has been very secretive about these findings. Even Chloe has few details of what the footage uncovered. Fred did tell Bradley that he's been talking to the local police and has since sent them some footage of dubious SUVs and peculiar men and women coming and going at odd hours of the night and early morning hours.

Much to my chagrin, in early December, Gina convinces me to deliver a fruitcake to the Hudson house as a ruse to find a way into their home and get some insight as to what may be going on over there.

The incoming HOA president, Sandra, also suggested this idea. She caught me last week pulling out my garbage cans and tried bullying me:

"Don't you think it would be a great idea to gift the fruitcake to the Hudson sisters? They rarely set foot outside of their home. Wouldn't it be a nice gesture from the community to bestow good graces upon them this year?" Sandra asked, while her chin hairs danced around as she spoke.

That woman really annoys me. Makes my skin crawl. Seriously, woman, do something about your face, I wanted to say.

"Gina," I plead, "I don't want to be part of this fruitcake exchange thing. I am, and have been, against it since Patty suggested it four years ago."

"Fred asked me to ask you. Come on, Holly, do this," she begs.

"Why me?"

"Well, you got the cake last."

"Yeah, but I gave it away. Susan, the UPS lady, should do it."

"No, Holly, we need *you* to get over there and invite yourself in."

"Technically, you should bake and deliver the cake, Gina. I know it was you who delivered

Larry's cake here. He delivered it to you. Then you dropped it off here."

"How do you know that?"

"Chloe told me."

"What? How did she know?

"Fred, the spy, of course. These days, Fred knows everything."

"Ugh . . . sorry, Holly, I panicked. I didn't want that fruitcake. It scared me."

"So you dropped it off here . . . to your best friend and mom of three kids, putting *me* in harm's way?"

"I'm sorry, the cake forced me into a frenzy. I was petrified. I'm sorry, I really am."

"A *cake* forced you into a frenzy? Where's Stephen King when you need him? *The Cursed Christmas Cake* . . . coming to bookstores near you this holiday season. Funny. Why does it have to be *me* to deliver the cake to the Hudson sisters?"

"No one else will do it. Also, you're the bravest of us all."

"I am? I beg to differ. You should do this."

"Well, I would, but they hate me. I reported them to Patty when she was the HOA president about their stinky trash. It smells like dead bodies, if you ask me. Their rancid trash is often full of rotting mangoes from their nasty trees—so they say. Also, there's something else."

"Something else?"

"Yeah, did you ever meet Dr. Davis?"

"No, why? Wait—Greta, Harrington, all the kids, and I went there one year for Halloween. One of my kids fell into his fountain. Never met him, though."

"Well, apparently, he went missing. Maybe the Hudson sisters had something to do with his disappearance. At least, Fred thinks so. Fred also thinks they have something to do with Harry's disappearance."

"Fred is also obsessed with watching the evening sky for evidence of aliens," I counter. "Has anyone talked to Harry about this?"

"Fred said Harry won't talk about it at all. He changes the subject."

"So now I have to put myself in danger? This is a job for the police, not me. How will *I* convince the sisters to let me in, anyway? How is this even possible?"

"You'll think of something."

"It's impossible," I say, shaking my head while my heart thuds loudly in my chest.

"Someone once sold a movie idea to executives about a tornado full of sharks. Nothing is impossible."

"Um, I don't know if I want to do this, and by the way, I really liked *Sharknado*."

"Come on, Holly, it's just a cake delivery. What could possibly happen to you? You can do this. Besides, Fred will film the entire exchange from the birdhouse."

I can see her frustration through her exasperated expression. She chews on her lower lip. She does this when she's frustrated. She changes direction. "Holly," she says, then hesitates. "I dare you to deliver a fruitcake to the Hudson house."

She's got me now. She knows me too well. "Alright," I mutter. "I'll deliver the stupid, shitty fruitcake and try to get inside. Challenge accepted," I say and immediately wish I hadn't.

"May the odds be ever in your favor," she smirks, using her announcer's voice. This, a *Hunger Games* reference. Funny, but also—not funny.

Chapter Forty-Two

Home
December 23–24, 2022
Dr. Davis

I t's been nearly a week since I was released from captivity. At first, everything in my home seemed like a luxury—ice cubes, television, air-conditioning, a warm shower, cool bedsheets, homemade gnocchi from Uncle Giuseppe's.

After a packed few days of sleep and self-care, I call Hope. I know that's not her real name, but it's what I'll call her, nevertheless. We speak on the phone for hours at a time. She helps me heal from my ordeal. Hope and I laugh and cry together, expressing both powerful emotions. We have established a deep connection through our shared experiences. This is a reminder that we are never alone in our struggles. Whether in moments of sheer hilarity or profound sadness, the interplay of laughter and tears can weave a beautiful tapestry of friendship. For this—for her—I am grateful beyond words.

We finally agreed to meet at my house.

In the moments before Hope arrives, I'm anxious. I long to see her again. I desperately need a break from my thoughts and the darkness lurking there.

When the doorbell rings, I rush to the door. Once opened, the sheer sight of her makes my heart leap. She stands there in a white summer minidress, looking like an angel. My angel. My hope. I reach out and hug her so tightly and linger longer than any other hug in recent recollection. The quiet fire brewing inside me since we met is finally unleashed.

Maybe because of her height—equal to my six-foot frame—I feel safe and warm in her embrace—my skin tingles. The joy emanating from my soul right now is so intense that I can't wrap my brain around any other comparison I have ever experienced in this lifetime.

"How are you doing? I mean, how are you really doing?" she asks sincerely as she pulls herself away.

"I'm trying my best to forge ahead, move on. But I'm having difficulty living with the past without reliving the past if that makes any sense."

"It makes perfect sense. I, too, still have vivid nightmares," she admits, trying to comfort me, but I find worry etched all over her face.

"I've got to tell you my real name," she offers. I should have told you before, but something stopped me."

"No. Stop! I don't want to know. You will always be Hope to me," I insist. "You are the only thing that kept me sane, keeping me going, surviving that day-to-day hellhole in there. You are what I asked for in the middle of the night when I was terrified of what could come next. I asked for hope. For that, I will always be thankful. I owe you my life."

"And I owe you mine. Saving you saved me. Does that make any sense?" She lowers her eyes to the floor.

"Yes, it does. Completely," I say, taking my hand and tilting her chin upwards.

Her eyes find mine, and in that gaze, I'm lost. I kiss her softly, hoping for a warm reaction. Such soft lips. I hoped she would melt in my arms. Instead, I melt in hers. She kisses my neck. I feel her breath in my ear. My ears are my sweet spot. She kisses my lips again, and we linger here until she breaks away and warns, "The desperate housewives in the neighborhood are swarming around your entrance by the gate. Empty-headed nitwits mulling around with their fake laughs and plastic smiles like extras in a movie. I nearly turned around and walked away, but I just had to see you. I need to be with you."

"Why are there people here?"

I move away to peer out the window.

"I guess they heard you disappeared and now have since returned, and you're the talk of the town these days. Even the old lady who hangs out in the park with her dogs has been walking by a few times a day, trying to catch a glimpse of you. There's even a reporter from the Treasure Coast News."

"I don't want to speak with anyone, let alone a news reporter. Tell him to go shit in a hat."

"Um, the reporter is a she, and, well, I never heard *that* expression before."

"You can count on me for your literary pleasure, my dear. I'm well-read, quite the Shakespearean," I say, trying to be clever. I'm feeling a little better now, and I can recognize a hint of my old self.

"You're funny." She smiles shyly. Her eyes twinkle. She has such kind eyes.

"There is something I need to tell you," I say. "Rather, something I need to show you."

"Sure, what is it?" Her eyes widen with curiosity.

I pull a key out of my pocket. "This key," I say. "This key is the key to the door of the room they kept me in."

"Where did you get that?"

"I found it. It was on the windowsill in my room."

"Are you sure it's the key to *your* room?"

"Well, not exactly. I never dared to place it in the lock. But I'm pretty sure. I hypothesize that a key is often left behind in case the captor one day becomes the captive. You know, plan B or a fail-safe."

"Hmm, I don't know anything about that. What are you thinking about doing with that key?" she asks, but I'm reluctant to tell her because I'm still unsure I can completely trust her. I never should have told her about the key, and now I regret that I have.

"You can't go back in there," she warns.

"Why not?"

"Well, you signed paperwork agreeing never to talk about it or go there unless invited. They could take your home, your money, your life even. Don't go back there. Please. You need to let it go. This thing that happened to you and me . . . it's bigger than just us. This has been going on for over two decades, maybe longer. It involves important people—very important people."

"Alright," I say, unsure I can let it go.

I know that there are other people in there. I need to rescue them. My thoughts run wild. While vigilante justice may work for some people, I remind myself that some people have died. This isn't right. I need to do something. I don't tell her my plan. I'm not even sure how feasible it is to sneak in and save anyone.

We agree to spend tomorrow evening, Christmas Eve, together. I lead her to the door and gently kiss her sweet cheek goodbye. I force a smile. Something deep inside tells me to tread lightly. I'm not sure I can fully trust her. My heart flutters and yearns for her against my brain's wishes. From everything I have experienced, witnessed, and learned these past few weeks, I know I must be better, do better, and rise to my highest good—evolve. However, as soon as Hope turns away and the door shuts, I begin to plot my revenge.

At six o'clock the following morning, I walk one mile toward the Hudson house. I feel dangerous all of a sudden. My bitterness steering me in a direction I should not take. As I pass the dog park, old lady Willa yells over to me, "Don't do it. It won't end well." Determined, I pretend not to hear the ranting of an old crazy woman.

I forge forward around the cul-de-sac and stand single-mindedly in front of the Hudson house. I close in, creeping my way slowly over to their basement window. I peer into the room I once inhabited and witness a man sleeping in the bed.

Stupid mistake; this window is visible to any snooping neighbor who dares to get close enough. The tinted window film is dark but not quite dark enough to obfuscate its inhabitant. I bang loudly against the window, but the man does not wake up. He was probably drugged.

I walk around the back of the house, climb seven stairs, and find the back door ajar. I slither in, silently tiptoeing to the door leading to the basement. Opening the door, my heart races ferociously, my head throbbing, but I continue down eight steps. The air feels heavy, and I can barely breathe. A panic attack is creeping over me slowly. I breathe in, breathe out, and focus on the task at hand.

At the base of the stairwell, the passageway is dim, too deficient of light to see a clear path forward. I feel my way down the hallway, tracing my fingers along the wall. I move slowly, tiptoe gingerly, as sweat trickles down my spine. My heart pounds so hard it hurts.

I take a moment to stand here silently, taking it all in. I'm petrified, but I take the advice of Eckhart Tolle in *The Power of Now*, the book given to me here while in captivity, and remind myself that yesterday has washed away, tomorrow hasn't unfolded, and we only have today. I embrace the "power of now" and forge ahead.

There are three locked doors down here. The one at the end of the hall on the left was my own previously. Since I know someone is in there for sure, I reach out and fiddle with the doorknob. Locked.

I use my key to open the door. Once inside, I call out in a strangled voice, "Hello?"

"Who's there?" The man lying on the bed sits up and looks over toward me. "Who are you?"

"I'm here to save you," I say.

"How did I get here? I don't feel so well," he says, then pukes over the side of the bed onto the concrete floor.

Luckily, he's not been shackled yet, and I'm able to put his arm around my neck and walk him out of the room. He's an older gentleman, frail, drugged, barely alive. I notice that his tan-colored shorts are stained with dried blood. One of his legs is stable; the other drags behind.

Before attempting our escape, I lean him against the wall in the hallway. I use the key to open the other two doors. One opens to an empty bedroom, the other to a semiconscious man.

"Hey," I shout-whisper, "I'm going to get help."

He looks my way and smiles. Then he throws an empty metal bowl in my direction. It hits my head, drawing blood from my brow. Then he falls over to his side. He looks pretty drugged up. I'll bet he thinks he's hallucinating. I wipe away blood trickling down the right side of my face, and I take the key to open the fourth door in the basement, but it won't budge.

"My name is Saul," the man I'm trying to keep upright offers. "Thank you for saving me."

"I'm Dr. Davis. We can't help anyone else right now. Let me help you get out of here, and we'll get help for the man in the other room."

We head down the dark hallway and steadily, quietly up the stairs, when I hear footsteps. Loud, heavy footsteps.

"Stay here on the steps. I will confront them. Do. Not. Move!" I demand.

But what will happen if I confront them? This is a dumb plan. I'm so amped up and stressed out at this point that I have to act. I should stand quietly in place, but panic is making me stupid when I need all my mental capabilities. Why didn't I bring a weapon with me?

I carefully open the door, surveying my surroundings. I look to my right, nothing. I look to my left—a large woman is waiting for me. Heavy, six feet tall, one hand on her hip, the other wielding an axe, a small one—a hatchet.

I panic. My mind fluctuates between fight or flight. A spike of adrenaline rushes in, and I race past her. She lets me. I race toward the front door. I hear old lady Willa's voice in my head. "Don't do it. It won't end well." I can also hear screaming coming from the basement.

She grabs my hair, yanking me back toward her. My legs give way from beneath me. Just before everything goes black, I see a pretty blonde woman at the front door, holding a cake. Our eyes lock. Silently, I plead with her for help. I'm hit with something hard, cold. I collapse onto the floor —blood trickles from my head, more than before, pooling by my face. I can't move. Now I can't see, then . . . nothing.

Part Two

The Aftermath:
Holly/Dr. Davis
2022–2023

Chapter Forty-Three

The Police Arrive
Christmas Eve 2022
Holly

A glimpse of bright lights flickering through the window can only mean one thing. The cops have arrived. I take a moment to collect myself. Breathe in, breathe out. My heart is still racing. Keep it together, Holly, I repeat over and over in my head. Keep it together. Stay calm. My hands shake. They're sweaty. I wipe them on my leggings. My hands continue to shake without my permission.

I open the front door and reach for the officer's hand, aching for some comfort or security. Help me, I say internally, feeling fragile. A damsel in distress, I am not, but I surrender today. I need rescue.

Charlie arrives just in time to collect the kids and shuffle them off to school. He looks past me to the children, whispering in my direction, "Call me if you need anything at all." I admire that Charlie never asks questions that are too difficult to answer. I nod in his direction and kiss the kids as they march toward the door.

"Mommy, why are the police here?"

"Can I stay here with you?"

"Can I hold the police officer's gun?"

"Am I in trouble?"

These are just a few of the questions my kids shout as they reluctantly head off to school with Charlie.

One of the police officers introduces himself.

"Hello, ma'am. My name is Officer Collins."

He offers me his hand. He stands before me, five feet ten or so, a patch covering his left eye. What happened to his eye? I wonder. Not the appropriate time to ask, obviously.

"May we sit?" he asks politely.

"Sit? Did you hear my 911 call? Someone was murdered at the Hudson house across the street. Shouldn't that be your first stop?"

"Yes, ma'am, another unit and ambulance are on their way. My partner, Officer Stern, and I are here to collect your story while it's fresh in your mind. Other officers will take care of the presumed crime scene."

"Presumed?" I roll my eyes in defiance. "I just witnessed a man bludgeoned to death with a hatchet! This is not a presumed accusation. And I still don't understand why you get here to talk to me before the police check the Hudson house, another unit or not."

"Please, ma'am, let's just sit briefly, shall we?"

"Alright." I give in.

We sit.

I'm jittery, and I say again, "Presumed?" I clench my teeth and tap my fingers on my leg.

"Calm down," Eye Patch says with cool, bland composure.

I'm immediately offended. I'm not some hysterical housewife. I feel myself getting hot internally.

As I glare at him, contemplating how I shall respond, Gina—who has already rushed into my house, through the foyer, and over to the couch, witnessing this exchange—spills out, "Let me give you a small piece of advice, Officer Collins. Never in the history of ever has telling a woman to calm down worked in a man's favor."

Gina's outburst is a gesture of affection. She looks out for me, and I always feel safe around her.

"Hello, Gina." Officer Collins stands and offers his hand. Gina stares at his hand. He returns his hand to his side.

"Hey," she says to me. "Are you okay, Holly? And what in the hell is going on around here?"

She sits and throws her arms around my shoulders for support.

"You two know each other?" I ask.

"Long story. Another day," Gina mutters quietly in my ear.

"What happened to your eye?" Gina asks the officer.

"A painful reminder never to turn a blind eye to crime," he quips.

"Are you trying to be funny now? Really? A man is bleeding out right now while you joke on my couch."

Not letting go of the eye patch, Gina says, "Don't tell me you went missing for a few days and returned with a missing eye like Harry is missing a finger?"

"Can we return to the murder I just witnessed, please?" I demand.

"Murder? Now you've got my attention," says Gina, pressing her hands between her knees.

"Ma'am, I'm going to record you if that's alright with you," says the other officer. "A recording will help us to better and more accurately report the alleged crime."

I want to scream out, "ALLEGED?" but I refrain.

"I think I should call the Chief. I'll have you know that Luke Junior is a very good friend of mine." Gina gives both officers a harsh look. "I don't think this is a good idea without a lawyer present."

"Let's just get this over with," I surrender.

Officer Stern starts the recording with my name, the date and time of day. I tell my story about delivering the fruitcake to the Hudson house. I give him the short version: I tell him I left my house at approximately 6:45 a.m. with a fruitcake to deliver to the Hudson sisters. I admit I had to provide the cake early in the morning because I had to shuffle the kids off to a Christmas celebration. This fruitcake thing …It's a tradition the neighborhood started in 2018. This year, it's my turn to deliver a fruitcake. When I reached the front door, I witnessed a man hit in the head with a hatchet. A large woman—I think it was one of the sisters—grabbed and hit him. He fell to the floor. I dropped the cake and fled back home, immediately calling 911.

Sirens blare in the distance. The ambulance and the other officers must have arrived. Gina grabs my arm and pulls me out the door toward the Hudson house, leaving the officers behind.

"Holly, never talk to cops without a lawyer."

"What? I didn't do anything wrong."

"Oh, Holly, nothing is ever what it seems. You can't just trust people because they are wearing a badge and brandishing a gun. You have to be careful. Also, how do you know those officers won't just erase the tape?"

"Gina, seriously . . . you sound like a conspiracy theorist right now," I say.

When we get to the Hudson house, all the neighbors have gathered around—nothing but silence from inside. The neighbors chatter, and I stay silent. Right now, I'm just a bystander. I turn around and notice that the two police officers we left behind at my house have already gotten into their police car and driven off.

"I told you something nefarious is going on in that house," Fred announces.

"You don't know the half of it," I say, but under my breath for only Gina to hear.

Harrington rushes toward us. "Hey, what's going on?"

I laugh out loud at Harrington's shirt. It reads *Does this shirt make me look bald?* That's just what I need right now.

"I love your shirt," I tell him.

"Thanks. Greta bought it for me for Father's Day."

Two stretchers clamor down the steps of the Hudson house, carelessly banging noisily at each step. The wheels are covered with remnants of the fallen fruitcake just outside the front door. Both bodies are covered with green blankets.

Someone standing before me cries, "The Hudson sisters are dead!"

Chapter Forty-Four

The House of Horrors
Christmas Eve 2022
Holly

A third stretcher follows the first two approximately ten minutes later. This gurney presents an unconscious man hooked up to an IV, his head bandaged, blood trickling down his face. Someone from the crowd yells out, "Dr. Davis!" but he is unresponsive, motionless. His right arm drops limp from the stretcher, and a key falls from his clutch as the wheels clamor past the final step. I snatch it, lickety-split, before anyone lays eyes upon it. I place it safely in the pocket of my leggings. Leggings are truly essential for every occasion. I smile to myself for the witty observation, even in these circumstances.

Two police officers and two other captives proceed down the steps. One, an older man, hobbles down the stairs, in bloodstained tan shorts, holding his private parts. He is assisted by a medic. The other, much younger man, saunters out smiling, waving to the neighbors, appearing high on drugs. His face and clothing, an orange jumpsuit, are spattered with so much blood it looks like the homecoming scene in the horror film adaptation of Stephen King's *Carrie*. The orange jumpsuit he is wearing is odd. Our zip code is printed on the front pocket.

The neighbors are all gasping, a cacophony of varying sounds from their sharp, inward breaths. Some are loud, others softer—an involuntary instinct we share for such an occasion.

Fred greets one of the officers at the foot of the steps. He offers to show the man his surveillance tapes. The officer scratches something on a notepad and hands Fred his business card.

Two other cop cars and a crime scene unit arrive, and now the house is swarming with police. A lady cop greets the crowd and asks everyone to head back home. She unravels a roll of yellow police tape and gestures toward another officer to help cordon off the area surrounding the home.

Chloe and Greta arrive just as the yellow tape unravels.

"Well, you missed all the fun," Gina asserts.

"We were watching it all unfold from Chloe's porch," says Greta. "I knew it. Some crazy mafia shit was going on in that house. Fred was spot on. Glad he taped it."

"I'm not so sure this is mafia-related. Greta, did you see all the men that came out of that house?

No telling what horrors they endured," I reply. "It was me that called 911."

"What?" asks Greta. "Spill it."

"When delivering the fruitcake this morning, I witnessed one of the sisters, the big one, hit a man with a hatchet. I dropped the cake, shattering it into a million pieces, and ran home as fast as my legs could take me."

"The haunted fruitcake," says Chloe.

"The haunted fruitcake," Gina and I awkwardly say in unison.

"Not funny," says Greta.

We agree.

I know it's inappropriate, but still, we can laugh a little because the pain of this day looms so large we need a bit of release.

"I witnessed a man get bludgeoned with a hatchet. I'm guessing the other men in the house killed the sisters trying to escape," I say, offering my hypothesis of the way this horror scene went down.

Luna arrives, seemingly out of nowhere, and says, "Did you know that your chances of meeting a murderer are less than one percent? How bizarre is it that we had one, maybe two, living right here in Laguna Palms? They say in your lifetime, the average person will only ever walk past thirty-six murderers."

"Okay, Luna, we don't know for sure if the Hudson sisters ever killed anyone, and that's enough about murder for today," pleads Chloe.

Rumors fly around the neighborhood about what could have transpired between the Hudson sisters and those three men to leave both of the sisters deceased, one captive with a head wound on a stretcher, one with a wounded crotch, and another covered in blood spatter.

"Time will tell," I say. "I'm sure we'll know soon enough. You know that no one can keep a secret in *this* neighborhood."

Later that evening, a lightning storm rolls in during the dead of night on Christmas Eve— deafening thunder and lightning strikes all around us from every direction. A bolt of lightning hits the front porch of the Hudson house amid a smashed fruitcake, a decimated cake plate, and yellow tape.

Gina, Greta, Chloe, and I rush to our porches and watch flames engulf the Hudson house as the firefighters arrive. My phone dings with a text to our group chat from Greta that reads:

> The haunted fruit cake strikes again [lightning bolt emoji] [cake emoji]

In the weeks that pass, very little is told about the horrors at the Hudson house. The incident is not reported in the newspaper or on television.

Judge Hudson, who was not living at the house then, had gifted the home to his daughters shortly after his wife, Esther, passed away. The judge was living in a condo close by. I assume that because this judge was revered in these parts, the story remains hush-hush amongst the police. Not a word spilled out of the station to us ordinary folk.

Gina, however, got the story from the officer with the eye patch. Because, of course, she did. Gina has her beguiling ways about her.

When my phone dings with a text message from Gina to our ladies' group chat, which someone has renamed Bitches & Booze—probably Gina—it reads:

> Mimosas at my house
>
> 10 am
>
> #Fruitcake

We all know that this ladies' get-together is not to be missed.

Chapter Forty-Five

The Truth
January 2023
Holly

Gina meets us at her front door with a restless smile and a tray full of mimosas at precisely 10:00 a.m. Gina is a stickler for guests arriving on time. We know better than to arrive even one minute late. This always seems to be the most difficult for me. I'm hardwired as a Latina on Miami time.

"You are never going to believe this shit," Gina says. "Hurry inside . . . so much to tell." She can hardly contain herself, giddy with excitement.

Once we are all settled on her supersoft, designer modular sectional, surrounded by oodles of beauty pageant trophies and framed cover photos of herself from famous ladies' magazines like *Elle* and *Cosmopolitan*, Gina says, "I'll start from the beginning."

We are about to spill out of our skin as we hang onto her every word.

Gina takes a sip of her mimosa, places it on the glass coffee table, and says, "Hold on to your britches, bitches. This is a story for the ages… In 1982, Judge Hudson, who was not yet a judge, meets his future wife, Esther, at a bus stop. He was working as a public defender and noticed a kerfuffle at the bus stop on his way home from the courthouse."

"Stop right there," says Greta with a smirk. "Kerfuffle?"

"Yeah, an old-timey word for an older timer. Pay attention." She continues, "Esther travels from Utah to escape some crazy family cult shit. The judge brings Esther home to his mom. She was just a teenager at the time. The Hudsons were known to help teens in trouble. They were a trusted family. The story has it that Esther's parents come looking for her, and AJ Hudson steps up and marries Esther so that she doesn't have to marry some old cult leader asshole."

"No way," says Chloe. "I've seen documentaries about these religious sects. Old men were marrying a stockpile of teenage virgins."

"Right. So Esther and his mom become friends, and they take in more troubled teens in the neighborhood. Only Esther has a dark side."

"Oh," "Ew," and "Ah," are our reactions all at once.

"This is getting spicy," I bite my thumbnail, feeling anxious.

"Esther has her husband build a prison of sorts in the basement. They call it a rehabilitation room for when the teenagers get a bit too unruly for Esther. Granted, ladies, this house has been right here in our cul-de-sac all these years, right under our noses."

"Okay, we know that. Go on," says Greta, getting antsy.

"Well, when one of their foster kids, or human rescues, disobey her, she punishes them with an eye for an eye kind of abuse. For example, one kid was caught sneaking out at night, so they swapped his sneakers for flip-flops. Next time around, they cut off one of his toes."

"No way that can be true. They would be arrested for child abuse," Greta insists.

"Hold on. This is the interesting part. All of these kids are grateful for their upbringing. Like, really grateful. So much so that years later, when they become police officers, lawyers, doctors, they send other troubled teens there for a hard kick in the ass."

"Holy shit," I say. "This is hard to comprehend. So what about Harry?"

"You are getting way ahead of me, Holly. Hold on. Patience."

Gina takes another sip of her mimosa and sets it back down.

"In 1993, Esther gets pregnant with twins. She gets the baby blues and never connects with her kids. She thinks the twins are a punishment from God for leaving her twisted cult. Adding insult to injury, Judge Hudson's mom dies the day the twins are born. A double whammy of God's wrath. She's convinced the twins are bad seeds. She neglects them."

"Double Whammy, indeed," I agree.

"Fast forward to grade school, and the kids get into trouble at home and school. One of them starts killing insects and animals. The other gets into fights defending her peculiar sister. The twins wind up spending most of their time in the basement prison. Their dad works a lot and is predominantly out of the picture, so only the twisted mom and psycho twins are at home. The kids get sent off to boarding school and college, but Esther puts them to work teaching lessons to other human rescues when they return. Crazy, right?"

"Were they kidnapping people around town? How did these people wind up at the Hudson house?" I ask.

"This I don't know, exactly. Eye Patch wouldn't divulge every little juicy tidbit."

"So what exactly happened to Eye Patch's eye, anyway?" asks Greta.

"I'm not sure. He wouldn't say, but I have my suspicions," says Gina.

"Maybe that's why he came clean with the story?" I assume.

"Maybe. Makes sense. A revenge of sorts to tell the story?" Greta offers. "Poor Harry. How did he end up there? What did he do? Who did he piss off?"

"No idea, but as the story goes, the twins, Trudy and Leigh, go bonkers when their mom, Esther, dies. Although Esther had a heavy hand, the twins took the punishment to another level. What is that old saying? Oh yeah, the apple doesn't fall far from the tree."

"Right," says Chloe.

"Where is the judge in all this mess?" I ask.

"When Esther dies, he gifts the house to the girls and lives in a condo close to the courthouse. He's supposedly unaware of the fiasco that has become of the Hudson house."

"Yeah, I don't buy that," says Greta. "Not one bit."

"Oh, one other thing," Gina continues. "He and his father were known to gift homes to their adopted and foster kids. The homes right here in Laguna Palms."

"No shit!" I say. This is fascinating. "Gifted?" I ask, just to be precise.

"Yes, gifted," says Gina.

"Like you were gifted your home from your dad? The same way that Chloe was gifted her home from her aunt?" I suggest.

"Not the same," Gina snaps.

"Really?" asks Greta. "How much do you really know about your dad and Chloe's aunt anyway?"

"I have no idea." Chloe's face looks confused. "I didn't know her well. I was surprised when her lawyer told us she left the house to us in her will."

Chloe places her head in her hands and begins to cry softly.

I hand her a tissue from my purse, and trying to break her from her apparent discomfort, I say, "I have more. The tissues in my purse are like my kids' questions—endless."

This brings a smile to her face. She pats her eyes with the tissue so she doesn't smudge her mascara, sits up straight, and spits out, "I'm sorry, everyone. I have been lying to you all. Please forgive me."

"What do you mean?" asks Gina.

"Well, my aunt gave us our house in her will. That much is true. What I never told you is that she was one of the Hudson foster kids."

"Why wouldn't you tell us?" Greta asks quietly.

"Well, honestly, I don't know exactly. At first, the topic just never came up. Then I was afraid to say anything when everything went down at the Hudson house on Christmas Eve."

"Why? Whatever your family background, we will always love you just the same," I say.

"Your poor aunt. I hope she was not tortured too badly living in that house," says Gina.

"The day we moved into the house, she left behind a Rubik's Cube on the kitchen table and a note that read, 'I hope you enjoy living here as much as I have. Love, Auntie Mable.'"

"A Rubik's Cube? That's strange. The police found many in the home of the Hudson sisters, according to Eye Patch," says Gina.

"Come to think of it, Luna said that Chet told her that his dad came home with one too." Chloe smiles now like a lightbulb just went off in her brain. "My aunt brought Luna different Rubik's Cubes when she was little. Then, as a family, we became really fond of them."

"Oh, crap. Talking about Rubik's Cubes, this belongs to you," Greta says, pulling a cube out of her beach bag. "Ava came home with it one day when Luna was babysitting, and I keep forgetting to return it."

Chloe responds, "She can keep it."

"And what about you?" Greta asks Gina. "What do you know about your dad?"

"My dad was raised here. His family moved here in 1984. When his mom died, he got the house but refused to live there. It was a rental until I moved in." Gina folds her arms and says, "No way my dad was involved. My life is not a thriller made for Netflix."

"You sure about that?" I'm joking, of course.

"And what about you, Greta?" asks Gina. "How did you come to own your house?"

"Um, we actually bought our house the old-fashioned way. We mortgaged the shit out of it and hope month after month I make enough commission to pay the bank, the insurance company, and the HOA and give Harrington the life he deserves until he can go back to his career designing and building high-rise hotels and bridges."

"Me too. We bought our house too. No connection to the Hudson house here," I declare playfully.

"Gina, you sent a text hashtag fruitcake," Greta says, wide-eyed, and I wiggle a bit, repositioning myself on the couch for another long story.

"About that," she says.

Suddenly, a loud knock comes at the door. Then the doorbell rings. Gina doesn't get up.

The door opens, and—holy shit—it's Patty.

"Where's *my* mimosa?" says Patty, standing in the doorway like a ghost. "I have medicinal needs."

Our eyes transfix on this woman who has seemingly risen from the dead.

"I thought you were dead," says Chloe.

"Well, you'd be wrong. How did you enjoy my son, Larry? Did you welcome him properly to the neighborhood?"

"Well, he was kind of a jer—"

Gina elbows me in the ribs before I can complete the sentence.

Still standing in the foyer, Patty says, "Larry moved out before I expected him to, after a fall down the stairs and a cryptic note from Harry."

"What? I'm so confused," I say.

Patty doesn't get the opportunity to answer because Greta is pissed off. Her face contorts with anger.

"I THOUGHT YOU WERE DEAD! The fruitcake! You have some explaining to do!" Greta hisses, one hand on her hip and a finger pointed in Patty's direction.

Patty waves her hand dismissively. "Don't wag your finger at me! I was poisoned. The cake was poisoned."

She slams the front door loudly and continues walking toward the couch. With her fancy designer purse in hand, flipping her hair back, and throwing her car keys on the kitchen island as she passes by, I realize that she is performing for us. You know, like for dramatic effect in a soap opera. This bitch is loving all of this attention. Does she think we're actors in an Agatha Christie movie? Ridiculous.

"I ate just a few bites of the fruitcake and felt woozy. I called rescue," Patty explains. "They found a Lego piece in my mouth, but it wasn't the Lego that did me in. It was the poison. I have learned that Leigh Hudson used strychnine powder, the main ingredient in rat poison, mixing the poison with opioids and confectionary sugar. She sprinkled the mixture on top of the cake. The rescue team shot Narcan up my nose to expel the poison and opioids. I threw up, shit myself, then passed out. I awoke in the ambulance, frightening everyone. I came back from the dead in my shit-soiled leggings. Fun times!"

"Not funny, Patty," says Greta, still furious. "I thought my daughter killed you by putting the Lego doggie in the fruitcake. You made me think she killed you! FOR YEARS! That's cruel, Patty!"

"I'm very sorry, Greta, but I, well, we—the police and I, that is—needed to get to the bottom of who would want to poison me. Also, the cake came from *your* house, and you're mad at *me*?

Initially, I thought *you* were the one that tried to kill me!"

"Me? Whatever for? Get over yourself!"

"Anyway," Patty continues, "I moved my son in while he was trying to get his shit together, and I worked with the police to find out who may have poisoned me. The only clue I had was footage of Leigh Hudson on my Ring doorbell, walking by my house on Christmas Eve. We didn't have much to go on, and the investigation got nowhere. In the meantime, I moved to Hobe Sound, and honestly, I didn't miss the neighborhood at all."

"Well, Patty, I feel personally offended," says Gina.

"Did you know about this?" I ask Gina.

"Only recently," she says.

Gina prepares a glass of mimosa for Patty and refills our glasses. We all take a collective pause and lean back against the couch cushions. Patty sets herself down near Chloe. Chloe instinctively moves over, not wishing to get too close to her. I can see in Chloe's face that she thinks Patty is a backstabbing, two-faced ghost bitch. Chloe would never say such a thing, but her face confirms it.

"This is a lot to take in," I say. "Patty, to be honest, your story seems a bit far-fetched. It's a farcical tangle of events if I'm being honest. You moved to Hobe Sound after being poisoned, and you're working with the police. I'm not so sure I believe this. It sounds ridiculous. Um, also"—I continue, on a roll now—"when you lived here, you spoke so much about the community taking care of each other. It was *you* who suggested the fruitcake exchange to begin with. Then you up and leave without a trace. No word from you for years!"

"I'm sorry. Really, I am," she tells us, but her facial expression says otherwise. Those words seem forced and fall flat. I suppose you never really know a person.

Chloe interjects, changing the subject from tensions swelling up within the room to some small talk about the neighborhood, some dumb new HOA rules, the new HOA hag, Sandra, and a story about the old lady in the park going off about a cursed fruitcake.

Patty reaches into her oversized Tory Burch tote bag and pulls out a leather-bound journal.

"What's that?" I ask.

"It's Leigh Hudson's journal. It was picked up by one of the officers at the crime scene. It was found in a locked room in the basement." Patty takes a deep breath and opens it. "There are excerpts in here about fucking with the neighbors. For fun."

"What?" asks Chloe.

The rest of us are captivated with bewilderment.

"She snuck in my back slider and poisoned my cake and made some snarky remark about stupid desperate housewives locking the front door but never the back sliders."

"*¡Ay, Dios mío!*" I swear. "That's right, I never lock the back sliders either," I admit.

"She also poisoned my son's cake in the garage refrigerator. From what it says in the journal, she mixed rat poison and opioids with powdered sugar, then sprinkled the sugar on top of the cake."

"Wait. Hold on! Larry was poisoned? I'm confused. We didn't know that," says Greta. "I know he broke his wrist falling down the stairs. He told us at the Super Bowl party."

"It says in the journal that she poisoned his cake. Larry told me he fell down the stairs after feeling dizzy after a shower."

"But what about Harry's uncle?" I lean in for the answer.

"What happened to Harry's uncle?" Patty seems surprised by the question.

"Harry gave his cake to his uncle, and then he crashed the car and died," Greta explains.

"I have no idea," says Patty. "Nothing in here about that. There is, however, something about a church fire she set off on Christmas Eve."

"Church fire? Oh no!" I shriek. "I gave my cake to Susan, the UPS lady. She said she was going to bring the cake to church with her. I wonder if it's the same church."

Before anyone can react, Patty blurts out, "Oh, and I learned one more thing from the police." She claps her hands together in excitement.

"What now? Jiminy Cricket!" Gina shouts.

"Jiminy Cricket?" That makes us laugh. "You really are on a roll with your old-timer words today."

"Well . . ." Patty pauses and stares into each of our eyes for added effect.

"Go on with it then," demands Greta.

"Alright. Within the locked room in the basement, the police also discovered small jars full of fingers and toes, a jar full of teeth, and one small jar with an eyeball, all floating around in formaldehyde."

At this point, everyone in the room gasps. I have no words, but Gina has many.

"Sounds like bullshit! Why didn't I know that? Eye Patch never told me about a locked room. You are grossly sensationalizing this tragedy."

"I am NOT!" Patty says defiantly.

I commiserate and observe to myself the obvious. On the outside, Patty is polite and polished, but look closer, and you'll find she has a dark side. She's way too excited about all of these disturbing details.

"Gina, Eye Patch probably didn't tell you about the room because . . . maybe . . . that eyeball is his?" Greta suggests like the proud member of the Scooby gang that she is. "No, really, think about it. I'll bet what Patty is saying is true. Chef at Drift and poor Harry are both missing fingers. Then there's Eye Patch. Makes sense."

"Someone needs to reach out to Harry," I suggest. "I'll bet he could use a friend right now with all of this going on if he *were* one of their prisoners."

"I'm texting Fred right now," says Chloe. "He'll round up the guys and head over there."

"Oh, one more thing." Patty again squeals in delight, eyes wide with joy.

"Oh, dear God," shouts Greta, then self-corrects. "I mean, oh snap! Snickerdoodles. We're sticking with old-timey expressions today. That's the theme, right?"

Patty continues. "I almost forgot about the letters. The police found letters, piles of them. The letters are from people, maybe their prisoners, confessing to some particularly atrocious, heinous crimes."

"Is there anything else?" asks Gina, looking bored with this whole charade. "I mean, allegedly.

I haven't heard anything about all the things you claim you know. But I'm determined to find out."

Greta adds, "My money is on . . . the public will never know any of these details if this story is true."

Patty concludes with, "It's true. I promise. Leigh, she was psychotic. Torture people by day, poison cakes on the holidays, and set off church fires for fun? Collected body parts like trophies, for Christ's sake! What kind of neighborhood is this? Glad I'm out!"

The other ladies and I lock eyes, and we concur.

Chapter Forty-Six

The Emergency Room
March 15, 2023
Dr. Davis

J udge Hudson arrives at the emergency room on March 15, 2023, at precisely 9:36 p.m. The rescue team races the gurney back into triage within seconds of arrival. I recognize him instantly. Judge Hudson, father to Trudy and Leigh Hudson. The sisters still keep me awake at night. Three months may have passed, but it still feels like yesterday. Leigh's maniacal smile, enjoying every moment she spent with me —pulling out my molars. That sick, ugly toad of a woman. Her sister, Trudy, attacking me from behind with a hatchet will haunt my dreams for eternity.

The fact that the judge finds himself during my scheduled emergency room rotation on the Ides of March is not lost on me. This, the seventy-fourth day of the Roman calendar, is marked as the deadline for settling debts. The day is also notorious as the day that Brutus and twenty-one other senators assassinated the tyrannical Julius Caesar. Brutus was the last to stab the dictator and send him to his tragic death, the quintessential turning point in Roman history.

Under my breath, I mutter, "*Et tu, Brute?*" And you, Brutus? Caesar never would have imagined a friend would betray him.

Two nurses walk past the curtain and inform me that he is having an acute heart attack. I took the Hippocratic oath, and for the love of all things Hippocrates: "First, do no harm." I know I should start treatment and adequately assess the patient. I should give him oxygen to help him breathe, nitroglycerine and morphine for pain, and maybe even perform an EKG. Instead, I tell the nurses, "Go on. I'll take care of him myself."

Pulling the cell phone from my pocket, I text Hope to explain that I'll get home a bit later than expected. I drag a chair from across the room, mainly for the dramatic effect of the loud metal scraping sound against the tile floor. I place his chart on the chair. Slow and steady, I lean over his bed, look into his eyes, and quietly say, "I know who you are."

He glares back at me, then looks away. Weak people can't keep eye contact. At this moment, I feel empowered. And for once in my life, I feel proud of myself. Dare I say…brave?

He looks back at me and admits, "I know who you are, too. I'm so sorry. I did my best with those girls."

"Did you? Did you have any idea what was going on in that dungeon?"

"I. Did. Not," he says defiantly, out of breath and barely alive. He grabs his heart with his right hand. His left hand is useless, unable to move.

"I have a short story to tell you, which may be the last you ever hear." I take a long, deep breath, trying to suppress the anger bubbling up in my chest. "When I was released from the hellscape of the Hudson house, I promised myself to return and help the other prisoners escape. So on Christmas Eve, I snuck in the back door, down to the basement, and unlocked the doors of the remaining prisoners' rooms with a key I stole while captive.

"I nearly died trying to free those men. I was bludgeoned nearly to death with a hatchet by your dear daughter, Trudy. Thankfully, Saul, the old man pervert with newly castrated balls, had rushed back down the stairs to collect the teenage drug addict, Tom. Tom, flying high, raced up the stairs, still drugged up, fearless, grabbed the hatchet by my head, and whacked your two precious daughters no less than twenty times each."

"I only wanted to help people, help kids in need." He spits out these words slowly and softly, barely able to breathe.

"You turned a blind eye to their behavior, the basement. You knew. You could have done something about this."

"I had no control over them. I was powerless." He looks away, hoping someone will waltz in at any moment and save him.

"Mr. Hudson, you are one of the most influential people in our community. People trusted you. You had the power to stop this. You were not powerless. No one takes your power. You give it away."

The judge sheds a tear. I can feel his pain. This was not the ending he wanted for himself or his family. I should have at least some empathy for him, but sadly, I have none.

In his last moments, he pulls himself together, sits up, and barks back to me, "Have you learned nothing from your time spent in your so-called dungeon?"

I push him back down on the gurney by his neck. My hands wrapped around his jowls, I lean over and whisper in his ear, "Oh yes, Judge Hudson, I've learned plenty. In the end, Judge Hudson,…we all get what we deserve."

I stand up straight and wipe my hands on my white coat. My hands feel dirty after touching his filth. I lean over his bed once again, stare deep into his eyes, and watch him die.

Out loud, I say, "Time of death, 9:47 p.m.," and mark it on his chart.

I wheel him down the hall, into the elevator, and down to the basement. Coincidentally, the staff in the morgue had already wrapped up for the evening.

I grab a tool from the counter, an eye plunger, and scoop out both his eyes. I place them in my pocket and tap on them, just as his daughter Leigh tapped hers after she pilfered my molars with the greatest of joy. I smile a large, comprehensive, happy smile. Feeling vindicated, I walk proudly away reminding myself to enjoy this moment. I fully embrace the 'power of now' and my brave ability to face and destroy my demons.

Chapter Forty-Seven

The Final Fruitcake
Summer - Fall 2023
Holly

As the months passed, the neighbors and I all lingered on in the neighborhood. Our bond is so close that moving away would be too painful. Friends come into your life for a reason, a season, or a lifetime; this lifetime would never be the same without them.

Old lady Willa was found dead in her bed on the first day of summer with no living relatives to grieve for her. The ladies and I had her cremated and sprinkled her ashes in the park she loved. Harry adopted her dogs. She may have been a bit batty, but neighbors should care for one another. However crazy, Willa was right about one thing. As she would say, I was the catalyst for change, the seeker. The delivery of my fruitcake uncovered the sins of the Hudsons in their house of horrors.

In the fall, Bradley and I decided to host a dinner party for our neighborhood friends. At precisely 7:00 p.m., Emmett greets the ladies at the door with a cocktail.

"Hello. Would you ladies like a cocktail? I will be your butter this evening." He memorized his line very well. I'm impressed.

"Cocktail? Yes. What is it?" asks Gina.

"Prosecco," he answers with confidence.

Gina grabs a few from his tray, handing one each to Greta and Chloe.

"What exactly does a 'butter' do?" asks Greta.

"A butter serves drinks to guests."

"Oh, you mean a butler," says Chloe. "You're doing a great job, my little friend."

"What else do butlers do?" Gina asks.

"Um, in the movies, they also answer the door and help old people put on their socks."

Just then, Luna pushes her way through the doorway, following the ladies, and chimes in, "Butlers also kill people sometimes."

"Really?" Emmett can't help but smile.

"Hello, kiddo. How about you and I get your siblings and go for a golf cart ride while the parents have dinner? Then we can go back to my house and watch a movie."

"Yes!" Emmett exclaims, drops the empty tray, and races to wrangle the others.

"Hurry," Luna yells after him. "Ana and Eva are waiting for us."

"Where are the guys?" I ask while picking up the tray from the floor. I'm curious why the girls hadn't arrived with them trailing behind.

"Harrington, Harry, and Fred will be here in a minute. They've been working on some new invention in the garage all day. Not exactly an invention, actually," Greta explains. "They're training Goldy to open the garage fridge and retrieve beer for them."

Greta hands me a white box from the bakery at Publix. Initially, it was a nice gesture, but once opened, the ladies let out an uncomfortable gasp. The fruitcake mocks us under the bright pendant lights hanging from the kitchen island.

"It's a joke," Greta insists.

We all stare at it and laugh reluctantly like a laugh was the correct response. But no one thinks this is funny except Greta.

"Ladies, it's a joke. I feel like we need closure. Well, *I* need closure. I just read the book *Normal People*, and—oh my god—the author ends the story randomly without wrapping up the love story, or lack thereof. I'm not okay. I like things wrapped up in a nice little bow."

"So, feeding us this fruitcake is wrapping things up in a bow?" I say while gesturing the making of an imaginary bow with my hands.

"In a way, yes." Greta shakes her bangs—a nervous habit.

We let it go and sit for dinner.

The men bore us with excruciating stories about fishing, chatter about football, and upcoming tee times. The ladies and I break away from the table as soon as we can safely escape the torment of overactive testosterone.

After dinner, while Bradley prepares Irish coffees for dessert, Gina says, "Come, ladies. I have presents for everyone."

"Presents, yippee!" An excited Chloe is first to sit down on the couch.

Gina pulls a photo out of her Marc Jacobs computer bag. "This is for you, Holly."

I am delighted to be the proud owner of an eight-by-ten glossy of Gina's feet, fire-engine red toe polish surrounded by Christmas holly.

"I love it," I say. And I really do love it. The photo is spectacular. "Gina, I must confess, the first day we met, I looked up treasure coast sugar toes—all one word—on feet finder dot com and found the *Birthday Feet* photo. It's been the screen saver on my Mac ever since."

"I'm flattered." Gina is actually blushing.

From her bag, she pulls out another photo for Greta. Her feet, this time, are surrounded by dog bones, with matching brown toe polish.

"I don't get it." Greta shrugs.

"Read the caption, silly," says Gina.

"Oh, Scooby Snacks! Ha! Thank you. I love it. I will frame it and put it in the hall closet where no one will ever see it."

"Very funny," says Gina.

Gina pulls out the final photo. It's Gina's feet surrounded by gnomes in a garden. Each toe is painted a different color.

"I know how much you love gnomes."

"These are my gnomes," says Chloe.

"Yes, I know. I borrowed them for the photo shoot, then returned them home, safe and sound."

"Thank you. I love it. I actually will frame this and put it in my foyer. It's lovely."

"You're welcome," Gina replies. "I love you ladies. I know we've all been through a lot lately, and I just wanted to say that you all mean the world to me."

"Gina, did you know Harry has your feet framed and hanging over his fireplace?" Chloe continues. "Fred told me. It's a photo of your feet in a white cooler surrounded by dead, bloody fish."

"Of course he does," I say. "Gross, though. Bloody fish?"

"Don't laugh. It's one of my most popular photos."

A crackle and a big boom shudders the house as thunder continues roiling closer. The lights flicker and black out completely. The house shakes yet again from a lightning strike nearby. Fred rushes off to the garage to check the breakers with Bradley. Harry grabs his phone to check his weather app for a thunderstorm warning or a tornado watch. The girls and I lock eyes in the darkness, and we panic.

"Oh no," I plead.

"The haunted fruitcake strikes again," Greta proposes with a hint of sarcasm. Greta grabs the cake from the island, and we follow her out the back door to the beach as the rain tumbles from the sky.

Once we reach the shoreline, Greta throws the cake into the ocean.

Suddenly, the rain slows, falling sparingly, the clouds dissipate, and a full moon smiles down upon us. The moon shines like a spotlight, busting through the clouds like a diva on stage. We watch the hungry waves consume the fruitcake, smashing it to bits along the shoreline.

We don't leave until every last raisin and walnut is washed away, devoured by the sea.

Gina grabs all of us in a bear hug and says, "It's going to be alright because we have each other.

Ride or die, ladies; we have each other. That's all we need."

"This is closure," I say to Greta, and we all agree.

I pull a key from my pocket and show it to the girls. "Oh, one more thing. I almost forgot about this. Here's the key I snatched from the sidewalk on Christmas Eve. It fell out of Dr. Davis's hand while he was whisked away on the stretcher."

"What are you going to do with that?" asks Gina.

"Throw it into the sea with the fruitcake," I suggest.

"Nope, I will give it to my friend Millie." She snatches the key from my hand. "You remember her from Pilates?"

"Of course," I say. "The seventy-plus-old teenage hippie with a rockin' bod."

"Well, she has this friend. His name is Randall. He collects keys with sinister backstories—an intriguing, mind-blowing tale for another time," Gina promises. "You'll love that story! He has so many keys and tales of secrets hidden along the Treasure Coast that he now stores them all in his friend's she shed.

"He collects wicked keys?" I ask and can't wait to hear all about that someday soon.

I look down, and there lies a brochure for Laguna Palms by my feet. The words jump out at me: Welcome to Laguna Palms, where your luxury and safety are in our secure hands.

I bend down and snatch it while reading the tagline to the ladies. We laugh. Then, each of us tear a piece of the brochure into tiny shreds and feed it to the ocean as the sea caps dance in the darkness.

Epilogue

Three Months Later

Gina was getting ready to dip her ebony-painted toes into a giant three-foot ceramic coffee mug filled with powdered cocoa mix and mini marshmallows when the doorbell echoes throughout the house.

Upon opening the door, Susan, the mail lady, smiles and hands Gina an envelope. "Hello, Gina. This is for you. I was told to hand deliver it."

"Thank you."

Gina sits on the couch with the manilla envelope stamped URGENT on her lap while her heart pounds. She takes a few moments to prepare herself to read the contents mentally. She traces over the scars left behind in the crook of her left arm with her pointer finger. This is the spot where the sweet needle would once deliver a warm rush of heroin. What started as a reprieve from the stress of runway modeling continued as an addiction to staying thin. The scars remind her of the life she left behind—thankful for the new life she has created for herself. She's grateful to the chief of police who looked after her when she was spiraling closer to death. She's most appreciative of the Hudson sisters' hard work put into her recovery. She combs her fingers through her hair. She recalls a humiliating memory. Leigh shaved her head—her punishment. Vanity. Selfishness. Weakness. She takes a deep breath and mutters, "Please let all this be over." Intrepidly, she tears open the envelope.

To my dear sweet sugar toes,
One of the men in my precinct just picked up a
teenager caught setting off dumpster fires. Since
the incident at the Hudson house, we've acquired a
new location. Additionally, I believe the time has
come to teach a certain Dr. Delicious a lesson or
two. My dear, it's time for you to produce a new
hologram. Are you ready to continue the mission?
Your biggest fan,
XOXO
—The Chief

The End

Enjoy a short horror story.

THE GIRL WHO COULD SEE
Tomorrow

LEAH ORR

What you choose to do today
will affect your tomorrows.

When the phone rang, I already knew who was on the other end. My heart sank, beating faster, and fear swelled in my chest.

"Hello, Mrs. Abrams, this is Ms. Riley from the elementary school."

"Oh. Hello, Ms. Riley. Is everything alright?"

"No, actually. Morgen is telling stories to other students in her grade, and quite frankly, she's scaring them. Can you come to school as soon as you can?"

"Please tell me exactly what happened."

"We can discuss it when you get here."

Yes, we will . . . but I already knew how this would turn out.

When I arrived at school, Morgen sat in the principal's conference room with a juice box and a chocolate chip cookie atop a square paper napkin.

"Mrs. Abrams, it's nice to have you here, and thank you for coming." Ms. Riley spit out the customary pleasantries.

I hugged my daughter and sat beside her, holding her hand for support beneath the conference table.

"Ms. Abrams, Morgen warned her friend Jessica on Friday that she would break her arm over the weekend. Jess did, in fact, break her arm at a soccer game the following day."

"Oh my," I said. Her intuition is getting stronger.

"That's not all." The principal continued. "A few weeks ago, she told a classmate his dog would die. Her stories are far too dark and scary for third graders. The kids are quite simply . . . well, they're afraid of her, and to be frank, I think we all are."

The principal paused momentarily, and I could see that what she was about to say would be uncomfortable for her.

"I think it may be a good idea to homeschool Morgen for the remainder of the year, and then let's re-evaluate in the summer months."

Although I wasn't surprised, this news still hit me like a ton of bricks. Knowing that nothing I could say next would change her mind, I was not about to try to explain my daughter's gift.

Instead, I said, "Okay. Thank you. We'll talk further in August."

I collected Morgen, her backpack, and the school essentials she would need for the remainder of the year. We walked out the door, never to return.

On the drive home, Morgen said, "Mommy, my friends at school have broken brains."

"What do you mean?"

"The kids at school can only remember the days before today, but they can't remember the days after today like we can."

"Not everyone has that gift, honey," I explained.

"Gift, Mom? It's not a gift. I don't want to know what happens to people tomorrow. It's distracting. I can't concentrate in class, because when I look at my teacher, I can see the flowers her boyfriend will give her tomorrow, or the dessert a boy at school will eat tomorrow. The things I see are random, usually uninteresting, and I don't know why only you and I can see them. I don't want to know everyone's tomorrows."

"Well, for now, it's probably a good idea to finish your second-grade studies at home, and I can teach you how to better tune out these images."

"What if what I see is bad, and I need to let people know so they can change the things they do tomorrow?"

"Honey, I don't think you can change a person's fate, and maybe it's best to stay out of it, even if what you see is very bad."

"What do you mean?"

"Well, let's just say you see that someone gets in a car wreck tomorrow, and you tell them not to get in their car tomorrow."

"Yeah?"

"Well, if that person stays home that day but gets in their car the next day, they may die the following day. Maybe it's their fate to die in a car wreck, no matter the day."

"But you don't know that. Maybe we have this gift so that we can save people."

"Maybe," I offered, but I wished she would take my advice not to get involved. "Morgen, the many times I told people what was about to happen to them, they didn't take my advice. They just thought I was nuts. They didn't come to me with a thank you when my premonition came true. They ran away like I was some evil witch."

"That's not fair."

"Life is not always fair, honey."

"I still think we were born this way for a reason."

"Maybe you're right. Sadly, I don't have all the answers for you," I admitted. "Can I ask, did your classmate's dog die?"

"Yes."

"I'm sorry. That must have been hard for you to tell him that."

"Not really. The dog was ancient. He's happier now."

"Happier? How would you know that?"

"I can see the doggie in heaven." She smiled and turned her face toward me. "Can't you see people and animals after they die?"

"No, not at all," I admitted.

I wondered if she could see the afterlife or if she was imagining a better life for those who have passed.

"Mommy, I already know that when *I* die, somehow, I come back to be with you again."

"Ok, now," I say, "No more talk about death please."

For the remainder of the year, I hired a tutor to homeschool Morgen. Sarah, just twenty-two years old, became quite a mentor for Morgen. The two of them worked for the first few hours of the morning. Then Sarah taught Morgen how to play piano, and they would end the day at the dog park or water park or with a bike ride.

When the school year ended, as Morgen packed for a six-week summer camp in Orlando, she said, "Mommy, you would be very proud of me."

"I am always proud of you, baby."

"I never told Sarah anything I saw."

"Good girl."

"I knew she would meet her boyfriend at a Taylor Swift concert, but I didn't tell her. I also knew the day before she got a phone call about a teaching job she wanted."

"So I need to find a new teacher for the fall then. Is that what you're saying?"

"I'm telling you this because I never told her anything that would happen, and I want to go back to school in the fall."

"Alright, but not the same school. I'll look into another school close by. Has it been hard for you not to tell Sarah everything you see?"

"Not really. A lot of what I saw were surprises, and I didn't want to spoil a surprise. Like, I met her boyfriend, and when I shook his hand, I saw him buying a wedding ring. I didn't tell her that. I wanted her to enjoy the surprise. But then a funny thing happened, and I was glad I didn't say anything."

"What happened?"

"He asked someone else to marry him."

"Oh no, honey. That's terrible."

"I know. But the following day, when Sarah was sad, I saw her meeting a new boy at the post office. He was really cute. I didn't tell her. I wanted her to be surprised to meet him, not expect it."

"You are turning into such a grown-up little lady."

"Thank you, Mom. I still can't help but think that I have this gift because I'm supposed to help people or save people. Maybe I'm *supposed* to help or save people from something really bad. Maybe if I can keep someone or some people alive long enough, they can change the world in a way only they were meant to—like superheroes."

"You are so sweet little girl. Only *you* would imagine saving super heroes so they can fix the world. How about this…if what you see is really bad and you think you can help someone or save someone, then do it. But if you feel that what you see can not help them or save them, then don't say anything."

"Okay mommy. I'll do that."

Four weeks after Morgen left for camp, the phone rang, and again, I already knew who it would be.

"Hello, Ms. Abrams. Everything is fine. Please don't be alarmed by my call."

"Alright." I let out a loud sigh. "What's happening?"

"Morgen saved two children this summer."

"How so?"

"Well, a few weeks ago, Morgen raced to the zip line and pulled her friend Janie off the chair. She said the line was frayed, and wouldn't you know it, she was right."

I gasped, although I was delighted she saved her friend.

"How is Janie now?" I had to ask.

"She's doing well. It was a scare for everyone, but we are all truly grateful that Morgen could see the frayed zip line from the ground level."

She thinks Morgen saw the frayed edges from the ground. I felt more at ease that they didn't know how exactly she knew about the frayed zip line.

The camp director continued. "Four days ago, Morgen showed up at the evening campfire with a fire extinguisher, which was strange, but no one questioned it."

"Okay," I said, bracing myself for the rest of the story.

"Well, one of the campers fell into the fire accidentally, and Morgen was there to spray her down with the extinguisher."

"Wow," was all I could say, suddenly at a loss for words. "Do you want me to pick her up?"

"Oh, no, Ms. Abrams. I just wanted you to know that your daughter has been quite the guardian angel around here for the campers. I am unsure if she is hyperaware of her surroundings or has premonitions. Whatever her talent, we are truly grateful."

"Thank you," I said. My mind was racing and wondering if we have this gift to help people, as Morgen suggested. Maybe I needed to rethink this.

A week later, I woke up in the early morning in a cold sweat. I saw Morgen choke on the pit of a cherry. Immediately, I called the camp. I got a steady buzzing sound. I checked my weather app and found that a thunderstorm was currently underway. The lines must be down. Although Florida is known for hurricanes, summer thunderstorms can be just as—or more—disastrous than a named storm.

I jumped in my car and drove the four-and-a-half hours to Orlando from Miami. I weaved in and out of traffic while rain pelted against my windshield, frequently rendering it challenging to navigate.

When I finally reached camp, Morgen was unresponsive in the nurse's office. When they told me what I already knew, that she had choked on a cherry pit, I couldn't hold back the tears and the pain in my chest.

She was rushed to the hospital, spent the remainder of the day in a coma, and died the following day.

While she used her gift to save two of her friends at camp, I was devastated that I had seen this coming and couldn't change her fate.

Years have passed, and I know I will never recover from losing my sweet Morgen. I have learned, however, that while we are all destined in some way to complete our earthly accomplishments or have lives we are fated to touch, the timeline can sometimes be manipulated. While I could not control my daughter's timeline for her exit point on earth, the lives she touched have forever changed the world.

One of the girls Morgen saved became a US peace ambassador, and the other won a Nobel Prize in Medicine for her work with skin grafts for burn victims.

Following Morgen's example, to honor her theory that we were blessed with this gift to help people, I walk the streets of Miami when I'm not at work. Occasionally, I get a hit, a hunch, about someone and warn people what I need to. Sometimes, I visit my new friend, Officer McDonald, at the police department about what may come.

One year later, I married Officer McDonald, my soulmate and best friend, and we are pregnant. I'm reminded of something Morgen once said to me.

"Mommy, I already know that when *I* die, somehow, I come back to be with you again."

I can only hope this precious baby I'm carrying belongs to the sweet soul of my Morgen.

Rubbing my tummy, I say out loud,

"Come back to me, baby girl, my superhero… Mommy's waiting for you."

The Fruitcake Cookbook

merry

Christmas

English Fruitcake

Ingredients:
1 pound mixed dried fruit
10 ounces brewed strong black tea
5 1/2 ounces unsalted butter
5 1/2 ounces dark Muscovado sugar
4 large eggs
1 3/4 cups all-purpose flour
1 tablespoon dark molasses
3 ounces brandy or sherry
1/2 teaspoon freshly ground nutmeg
2 teaspoons freshly squeezed lemon juice
1 teaspoon baking powder
4 ounces ground walnuts
8 ounces glacé cherries, halved
8 ounces candied orange peel, coarsely chopped

Prepare:
The day before baking, place the dried fruits in a large bowl. Add the tea and stir well. Cover and let sit at room temperature overnight.

Line the bottom and sides of a greased 8 x 3-inch round cake pan with parchment paper.

Place the butter and sugar in a large bowl and whisk with a fork until the mixture is light and creamy. Beat in 1 egg, then beat in 1/4 of the flour. Repeat until all the flour and eggs are used. Add baking powder, molasses, brandy, nutmeg, and lemon juice. Stir gently.

Drain the dried fruits and add the chopped walnuts, cherries, and candied peel.

Add the fruit mixture to the cake mixture. Fold in gently.

Spoon the batter into the cake pan. Bake for 2 1/2 hours at 325°F or until dark golden brown. Cool for 40 minutes.

Add vanilla icing and confectionary sugar to decorate if so inclined.

Italian Fruitcake - Panettone

Ingredients:
4 teaspoons warm milk
1 teaspoon dried yeast
8 teaspoons sugar
2 sticks butter
5 large eggs
2 teaspoons vanilla extract
Grated zest of 1 lemon
Grated zest of 1 orange
3 1/2 cups flour
A pinch of salt
7 tablespoons raisins
1/2 cup toasted hazelnuts chopped
1/2 cup dark chocolate shavings
3 tablespoons rum extract
8 tablespoons candied lemon and orange peel,
finely chopped

Topping:
1 teaspoon egg white
1 teaspoon powdered sugar

Prepare:
Grease a panettone pan with softened butter.

Place the warm milk in a bowl and add the yeast
and 1 tsp of sugar. Mix well and leave for a few
minutes.

Put the remaining sugar in a large bowl and beat with the butter and vanilla extract, using a hand mixer, until light and creamy.

Add lemon and orange zest and mix. Add the eggs a little at a time until all are well incorporated. If the mixture starts to curdle, add a tablespoon of the flour and beat in with the eggs.

Place the flour in a large bowl, mix with a pinch of salt, and make a well. Add the yeast mixture, then the butter and egg mixture, folding in with a large spoon to make a soft dough.
Knead for 5 minutes in the bowl until the mixture starts to come together and is pretty sticky.

Put the dough onto a floured surface and knead for 10 minutes until everything has come together and you get a soft, stretchy dough. Add a light sprinkling of flour to the surface and your hands as you go to stop the mixture from sticking.
Place in a lightly greased bowl and cover with plastic wrap; keep in a warm place for 2 hours or until it doubles in size.

Place the raisins and chopped hazelnuts in a small saucepan with the rum extract and heat on low for about 5 minutes or until the fruit has absorbed the liquid; set aside to cool.

When the dough rises, tip it onto a lightly floured surface and knead for another 5 minutes. Gradually knead in the soaked raisins and chopped candied peel. Shape the dough into a ball and pop it into the prepared panettone pan. If using an 8-inch deep cake pan, wrap a layer of baking parchment around the outside of the tin to come up about 2 inches above the rim, and secure the paper with string. This will help contain the dough as it rises.

Cover lightly with plastic wrap and leave to rise for another hour until it has risen to the top of the pan or paper.

Preheat the oven to 350°F.

Mix the icing sugar and egg white and gently brush over the top of the panettone. Add chocolate shavings.

Place the panettone in the oven and bake for 50–55 minutes or until golden and risen. Insert a skewer into the middle of the cake to test if it is done.

Leave to cool completely.

Cut into wedges to serve.

Pineapple Fruitcake

Ingredients:
3/4 cup butter
1 cup white sugar
2 eggs
2 cups all-purpose flour
2 teaspoons baking powder
1 teaspoon salt
1 teaspoon almond extract
3 cups golden raisins
1/2 cup candied cherries
1 cup candied mixed fruit peel
1 (15-ounce) can of crushed pineapple with juice

Prepare:
Line an angel food pan with parchment paper and brush with melted butter.

Cream butter or margarine, and then beat in sugar. Beat in eggs one at a time, beating well after each addition. Stir in extract. Mix in flour, baking powder, and salt. Stir in raisins, cherries, pineapple, and mixed peel. Cover bowl and let sit at room temperature, 8 hours to overnight.

Bake at 300 degrees for 2 1/2 hours with a pan of hot water placed on the lowest rack of your oven during baking. Brush the warm cake with some melted butter.

Leave to cool completely before adding cream cheese icing and/or confectionary sugar.

Chocolate Fruitcake

Larry didn't actually bake this cake. He bought a chocolate cake with sprinkles from Publix. It was most likely not a fruitcake at all.

Havana Fruitcake

Ingredients:
4 ounces candied red cherries
4 ounces candied green cherries
4 ounces candied orange peel
4 ounces candied citron
4 ounces candied pineapple
1 cup raisins
1 cup unsweetened flaked coconut
1/4 cup aged rum, plus more when cakes are baked
1/4 cup coconut rum, plus more when cakes are baked

For the cake batter:
1 cup unsalted butter at room temperature
1 cup granulated sugar
1 cup light or dark brown sugar
2 teaspoons baking powder
1 teaspoon salt
1/2 teaspoon cinnamon
1/3 teaspoon nutmeg
Zest of 1 large orange
4 large eggs
3 3/4 cups all-purpose flour
2 tablespoons unsweetened cocoa powder
1 cup pineapple juice

You will also need:
4 small or 2 large loaf pans. You could also use a bundt cake pan or two small 10-inch cake pans.

Directions:

In a large bowl, combine the candied fruit with raisins, coconut, and both kinds of rum. Stir well to combine, and soak for 30 minutes.

After 20 minutes, preheat oven to 325°F. Grease and flour your pans, and set aside. Combine the flour and cocoa powder and set aside.

In another bowl, cream together the butter with both sugars. Mix in the baking powder, salt, cinnamon, nutmeg, and orange zest. Mix in one egg at a time. Gradually mix in the flour mixture, alternating with the 1 cup of pineapple juice. I like to mix in 1/4 of the flour, then mix, then add 1/4 of juice, mixing in between each add-in. Fold the candied fruit mixture, including any liquid/rum, into the batter until well incorporated.

Divide batter into the loaf pans, bundt pans, or cake pans. Bake for 40 minutes or until the knife comes out clean from the center of the cake. Remove from oven and cool slightly. Drizzle rum on top of each cake, just enough to wet the tops. Seal the foil closed and let the cakes sit overnight. The next day, wrap the loaves tightly in plastic wrap and store them in the refrigerator until ready to serve.

Decorate:
Holly added cream cheese frosting, Hershey's chocolate syrup, and sliced strawberries.

Indian American Fruitcake

Ingredients:

Fruit mixture:
1 cup rum
1/4 cup cranberries, dried
1/4 cup raisins
1/4 cup dates, chopped into bite-sized pieces
8 ounces of cherries, pitted and halved
2 small apricots, pitted and chopped into bite-sized pieces
1 cup almonds
1/2 cup hazelnuts
2 tablespoons sugar
2 tablespoons pure vanilla extract
1 teaspoon almond extract

Cake mixture:
12 tablespoons butter
1/2 cup brown sugar
1/2 cup sugar
2 large eggs
1/2 cup goat milk
2 cups flour
1 teaspoon baking powder
1/4 tablespoon cinnamon

Prepare:
Preheat oven to 350°F. Grease a 10-inch pan or bundt cake pan.

Warm the rum in a small pot over medium heat. Place the cranberries, raisins, and dates in a small bowl, pour the rum over the fruit, and set aside.

Combine cherries, apricots, almonds, hazelnuts, sugar, and extracts in a large bowl and toss well. Set aside.

In a mixer, cream the butter and sugars on medium speed until light and fluffy, about 2 minutes. Add the eggs and milk on low speed. Add flour, baking powder, and cinnamon.

Drain and reserve rum from the fruit mixture, and add to the mixing bowl until the fruit is evenly distributed.

Bake for 45 minutes. Poke a hole in the cake with a toothpick and pour leftover drained rum on top of the cake. Let cool before removing the cake from the pan.

Book Club Topics & Questions for Discussion

The story sprinkles in a bit of Roman history. The fruitcake's origin, the panettone's love story, and Caesar's downfall are highlighted in this story. What can we learn from the Romans regarding love, war, and enemies when it comes down to human nature's lust for power, pride, and greed?

Life is full of contradictions. Order versus chaos. Sometimes, you need chaos to create order in your life. Tell a story about a time when something unexpected happened in your life and the good that came from it.

Esther gets a letter from her mom and dad inferring that her life would be fraught with strife for leaving her religious community and her obligation to marry the pastor. She believes her girls were born evil—a punishment from God. Do you think people are born evil or driven to do bad things due to their poor upbringing, neglect, abuse, etc.?

What do you think happened to the chef's ring finger? Do you think he may have been a prisoner at one time at the Hudson house for his adultery? What do you think really happened to Officer Collins's eye and Harry's pinky finger? Coincidence?

Esther punishes some of her unruly foster kids in the basement. Do you think Trudy and Leigh learned to physically punish their prisoners from their mom, or do you believe they escalated the punishment once their mom died?

Bradley tells Holly that he doesn't trust anyone who hasn't had their heart broken in all the right places. As a music producer, he appreciates that pain elicits art. Have you ever created something artistic that was produced from pain?

Why do you believe the judge allowed Esther to punish the children in the basement?

Do you believe that turning a blind eye to injustice is just as bad as the act itself?

Hope chose to accept her fate, while Dr. Davis decided to seek revenge. How do you feel their actions fit into gender, societal, or professional roles?

In the end, Dr. Davis sought revenge instead of repentance. Do you think he will continue to aid and abet the murder of his patients? Or do you think he will become a better doctor after reflecting upon all of his past indiscretions?

In some instances, the fruitcake tragedies were brought on by Leigh. In other instances, the fruitcake's appearances brought about disasters from other-worldly events. Examples include Uncle George's accident, the lightning fire at the Hudson House, and the power outage at Holly's House. Could the Native American's curse actually be affecting the fruitcake exchange in Laguna Palms? *Could* the fruitcake be haunted?

The author references Millie and Randall from her book, *The She Shed.* Do you or don't you like when authors place what are commonly known as "Easter eggs" in their books?

How well do you *really* know your neighbors? Which ones do you trust? Which seem sketchy? Why?

Other Books by Leah Orr:

Historical Thriller:

The She Shed

Murder at the Opulence Hotel:

The Executive Suite (Book 1)

The Bartender (Book 2)

The Champagne Toast (Book 3)—coming soon

Horror Shorts:

The Old Lady in the Gazebo

One Wish

The Last Mile

Till Death

A Squirrel Named Santa

The Girl Who Could See Tomorrow

Children's Books:

A Child's Wish—coming soon

Messy Tessy

It Wasn't Me

Kyle's First Crush

Kyle's First Playdate

Summer Beach Fun—Coloring book for kids

Coming Soon . . . Book 3 in the Murder at the Opulence Hotel Series

LEAH ORR

The Champagne Toast

Keep in Touch

 facebook.com/leahorr

 instragram.com/leahorr723

 goodreads.com/author/show/
21341008.Leah_Orr

 amazon.com/kindle-dbs/entity/author/
B002BLWXFG?

 Find me: LeahLu

A Note from Leah

Dear Friends,

Thank you for reading *The Fruitcake* and spending time with some of the people in my head. I hope you enjoyed this twisty mystery, and I hope these characters were as real to you as they are to me.

I would be very grateful if you would take a moment to write a short review on social media and help promote this book to your friends, family, and followers, as it may expose new readers to my books. I read every review. Since you took the time to write it, I take the time to read it. All of the profits from the sale of this book are happily donated to the Cystic Fibrosis Foundation.

To keep in touch or inquire about discounted copies of this book for your book club or signed copies, you can email orrplace1@bellsouth.net or contact me through my website at www.leahorr.com. You can also follow me on Facebook, Goodreads, and Amazon.

With great gratitude,

Leah

Special Thanks

A special thanks to my brother Rico for the genesis of this story. Thank you, Holly Kelly, for allowing me to partially steal your identity. Thank you to Edith Cimino and Dave Salomon for help with Holly's Latina commentary. To Kim, Donnie, and Kaitlyn Brown for the inspiration for characters Fred, Chloe, and Luna. Thank you to my editor, Anna Roberts. I truly appreciate you. To Kathryn Michael, my beta reader, for helping me decipher which loose ends to tie up and which to leave with the reader. To Moon, for your help with Holly's song melodies for the audible version. To my mom, Josephine Lepore, for her fruitcake art and help with the first and last round of edits. Finally, to my husband for the countless hours I spent typing on the computer, not paying any attention to "all the things" you believe I heard you say. In my defense, these characters speak so loudly in my head that making space for real people is sometimes challenging.

About The Author

Leah Orr is an Amazon #1 best-selling author. She lives in Jensen Beach with her husband and three daughters.

Leah donates the profits from her books to the Cystic Fibrosis Foundation to help find a cure for her youngest daughter and other children whom are afflicted.

Gift a digital or paperback fruitcake this holiday season or the next special occasion with family or friends.

https://www.amazon.com/Fruitcake-twisty-murder-mystery-forget-ebook/dp/B0CHWHRH7R

<u>Did you know?</u>

December 27th is National Fruitcake Day.

Manitou Springs, Colorado has an annual Fruitcake Toss
Competition in January every year at Memorial Park.

Romans brought fruitcakes to battle for nourishment.

A pineapple fruitcake was brought to the moon on the Apollo
11 - but was not eaten.

Every British royal served fruitcake at their wedding until
Prince Harry— who broke the tradition.

In the 1800s it was customary for unmarried wedding guests
in England to stick a slice of fruitcake under their pillow so they
could dream about their future spouse.

The oldest fruitcake was found in an Egyptian tomb and
guesstimated to be over 4,000 years old.

Fidelia Ford of Michigan baked a fruitcake in 1878 and it's
still being passed around the family to honor her legacy.

Trappist Monks, of Assumption Abbey Bakery, in the
Missouri Ozarks sell 20,000 fruitcakes a year.

The Claxton Bakery in Claxton, Georgia makes
4 million pounds of fruitcake a year, and Claxton is
considered to be the fruitcake capital of the world.

The Traveling Fruitcake

Sign your name below and where you're from,
then pass it on.......